TRAILING TENNESSEE

CORY WHEELER MIMMS

Library of Congress Cataloging-in-Publication Data

Mimms, Cory Wheeler.
Trailing Tennessee / by Cory Wheeler Mimms. -- First edition.
    pages cm
Summary: After his father's sudden death, fourteen-year-old Eli Sutton begins
hiking the Appalachian Trail, a dangerous trek on which he is pursued by park
rangers and spirits, to fulfill his dream of reaching Mount Katahdin and carving
his initials on the same tree as his father and grandfather.
ISBN 978-1-940052-00-7
[1. Hiking--Fiction. 2. Appalachian Trail--Fiction. 3. Runaways--Fiction.
4. Spirits--Fiction.] I. Title.

PZ7.M649Tr 2013
[Fic]--dc23

                        2013016980

CRAIGMORE
CREATIONS

2900 SE Stark Street, Suite 1A
Portland, OR 97214
www.craigmorecreations.com

"The woods are lovely, dark, and deep..."
Robert Frost

Eli Sutton sat near an oak grove. He leaned against a rock and ate oatmeal for breakfast. Morning sun reached through the trees and touched his face. He blinked and traced the sound of a bird's call. A few crows drifted overhead, circling and waiting for Eli to leave so they might snatch up any bits of food he left behind. Birds will be birds, Eli supposed.

Eli stood. A twig on the fire cracked and spat over the ring of rocks he'd arranged the previous night. He pressed his heel into the coal. Raising his boot, he saw the ember and dirt mix together, the earth swallowing the earth.

He rinsed the oatmeal from his pot in a pail filled in a nearby spring. The water poured from the earth cold and clean, but Eli boiled it before drinking. His father had warned him some water contained bacteria that could make people sick. A sure way to kill it was to boil it. He put the pot in his pack and opened his canteen. He filled his mouth with water, sloshing it around to get the oats unstuck from his teeth. As he swallowed, he heard something rustle behind him.

A red squirrel ran along a branch and down the trunk of a tree. Its long tail bounced as it went. It dropped to the ground and began scratching for fallen nuts, plucking them from the twigs and dry leaves with fury paws.

"Are you a skin-walker?" Eli asked.

At the sound of his voice, the squirrel's ears twitched and it stopped scavenging. Its fur bristled and then froze. The long hairs growing from its ears stood straight up, and it watched Eli with dark eyes rimmed with light brown fur.

Eli remained motionless and the squirrel did the same. Time stretched around them. Eli felt the earth pulling against the soles of his boots, pulling him down like a magnet and rooting him in the soil. He wished he could turn into a squirrel and live in these woods. He would spend his days scrounging for nuts and berries and his nights curled in a warm den.

A tufted titmouse landed in the tree behind the squirrel. It called several times, paused, then called again. Its voice opened Eli's ears. To be a bird would be better. To let the wind carry him above the forest, above the smell of moss and campfire smoke—into the canopy. The leaves moved in the wind and became a golden-green river, flickering with shadow and light and swimming with insects and animals. Eli imagined a school of rainbow trout drifting among the leaves, jumping into the sky, snatching dragonflies in flight,

6

and splashing back into the canopy. The air crept through his shirt and cooled his skin, drawing him down from the sky and his imagination.

The titmouse had gone, and the squirrel had resumed eating the acorn it held. The air trickled through its deep red fur and swirled the loose leaves on the ground. Eli reached into his pack and took out a handful of trail mix. The squirrel continued eyeing him and eating. Eli tossed a few pieces of trail mix on the ground. After a moment, the squirrel sniffed and crawled toward the food. It stopped every few inches and stared at Eli. Its whole body bobbed with the beating of its heart.

"I'm not going to hurt you," Eli said.

Stretching its neck out, keeping its distance, the squirrel nibbled at the nuts and dried berries. It grabbed a peanut in its teeth and darted back toward the tree.

Eli laughed and turned back to the fire. He spread out the remaining embers with a branch. Ash and smoke billowed into the air. He tossed a bit of soil into the hole with his camping shovel and threw the ring of rocks back into the forest. His father had taught him to leave no trace while camping.

He dug in his pack and pulled out his wrist rocket. He felt the texture of the grip, his fingers sliding into place. He pulled on the sling a few times. The rubber stretched and transferred its tension onto his arm. He set the slingshot down and searched the ground, looking for marble-sized stones.

He discarded several that were too big or too jagged. Good ammunition was as smooth and round as possible. A few yards away, there was a pile of large rocks. He could probably find little ones near them. He stepped through the grass.

Suddenly, he heard a buzzing noise. Before he knew what it was, he saw the earth under him move, slither.

Eli's body reacted before his mind. He jumped into the air, dropping the few stones he had collected, as his adrenaline rushed. He didn't see the rattlesnake until it struck, its head slapping against his boot, its fangs squirting venom. Eli landed in the dirt and scrambled away. The snake turned and disappeared into the grass.

Eli's heart shook his chest. His eyes darted through the grass, checking for other snakes. He stood up and inspected his boot. He didn't feel any pain in his foot, but he couldn't be sure. He trotted back over to his pack and unlaced his boot with shaking hands. He tore off his sock and examined his foot. There were no marks.

Eli took a deep breath and shook his head. He was several miles from home. He might not have made it back to his house had the snake's fangs penetrated the leather.

He pulled his boot back on and tightened the laces. He grabbed a few misshapen rocks and stuffed them into his pocket. They would have to do. He pulled on his wrist rocket and loaded one of the rocks into the sling. He took aim at a branch and let it fly. The rock whizzed off target but still smacked the tree trunk with a satisfying crack.

With his ammunition in his pocket and his heart returning to a normal beat, Eli picked up his pack and turned for home, a small house on the edge of the Cherokee National Forest.

Dee set her phone on the kitchen table. "I'm worried about him, Sam," she said. "I can't help it. I'm a mother." Beyond the window, the thick forest of the Appalachian Mountains stood tall. The trees were like soldiers forever at their stations. "He's out there all alone. You know I don't like that you let him go out there alone. He's just a boy. All I ask is that he calls before night and in the morning. Why did we buy him the phone if he isn't going to use it?"

Sam glanced at his breakfast. "He's fine, Dee," he said as he pushed his eggs around his plate. "By his age, I'd spent much longer than a single night camping alone in those woods."

"Eli isn't you, Sam," Dee said.

Sam put down his fork. "I didn't say he was. It's just— well, you baby him," Sam said. "You treat him like a little kid, and he's not."

"He's only fourteen," Dee said. "He is still a kid."

Sam stood and set the plate in the sink. "Just give him some freedom. What's the harm? He's just tromping around in the forest."

Dee sipped her coffee and stared out the window. She hit the speed dial on her phone. Eli's number appeared on the screen. The ringtone danced in her ear, and then the voicemail picked up: "Eli's phone. Leave a message." Simple and sweet. Dee's message wouldn't be. "Eli Sutton, you better call me as soon as you get this. You're in big trouble. You better hope a bear got you because that's the only thing that'll save you from my wrath when you get home." Dee paused. What if a bear had attacked him? What if he was out there in the woods mauled to death? Her voice softened. "Eli, call me, baby. Turn your phone on and call me like we agreed. And you better have eaten all the food you took, too. I know you like to feed the animals, but that food is for you." She set the phone down. A breeze blew through the trees outside, shaking the branches.

Dee stood and washed the breakfast plates. She opened a can of dog food and scraped it into a dish. "Come here, Pepper," she called. "Come get some breakfast."

She sat on the porch and flipped through a magazine, never getting more than a few sentences into any of the articles before her mind turned back to Eli. She tossed the magazine aside and looked at Pepper, who lay in the sun. "Nothing ever worries you, does it, Pepper?" Pepper's ear twitched at the sound of her name. Dee let her gaze drift off the porch, into the hills. Birds sang and the leaves swayed in waves of wind.

Two hours later, Eli walked out of the woods wearing his pack and whistling. Dee's shoulders relaxed and the creases in her forehead smoothed as she watched him. His features were changing. The soft cheeks hardening. He may not be an adult yet, but Sam was right; he wasn't a little kid anymore. He was thin and getting taller every day, becoming more like his father. Acting like him, too. They both loved the outdoors. They loved fishing, hunting, hiking, spending time among the trees and insects. Dee supposed it came from Eli's grandfather, Jack. Jack had been a man of the wild, a hard-working man, and a man who knew how to enjoy life.

"How come you didn't call to check in?"

Eli's head snapped up at the sound of his mom's voice. "I forgot," he said. It was the truth. He'd forgotten that he even had the phone in his pack, sealed in a plastic bag and tucked in a pocket.

"That's it then," his mom said. "You're not going back out there. I told you that you could go only if you called to check in. I've been worried all night long."

Eli climbed the porch stairs without saying anything. Fighting his mom would just make things worse.

"Take those muddy boots off before you go inside, too."

Eli sat on a chair next to his mom and unlaced his boots. The boots had been a gift on his fourteenth birthday. They were still getting broken in and they might have just saved his life. That was a story he would keep to himself. If he told his mom about the snake, she might never let him go camping again. He pushed the boots under his chair and stood.

His mom wrapped her arms around him and kissed him on the forehead. "It worries me so much to have you out there alone," she said.

"I'm sorry I forgot to call," Eli said, returning his mom's hug.

"I love you, Eli." She squeezed him again.

"Okay, okay, you're going to suffocate me." Eli pushed her away.

His mom laughed and held him at arm's length. She brushed his sloppy brown hair out of his face. "You're getting so tall," she said, smiling. "Now, make a sandwich for lunch and then help your father. He's in the garage fixing the mower."

"Still?" Eli asked. "I thought he started that days ago."

"Well, it's a complicated job, I suppose."

Eli walked into the kitchen, Pepper following at his heels, her nails clacking on the floor. He ate a handful of trail mix and a banana and went into the garage. His father hugged him. He smelled like grease and oil.

"How was the woods?" he asked.

"They were good," Eli said. "I think I saw a skin-walker."

His father laughed. "You sound like your grandfather. Next you'll be telling me the Raven Mocker is coming to get me."

Eli shuffled his feet and looked at his hands. His grandfather had been a tall man with swollen knuckles and meaty fingers. His hands were old gloves, well-worn, and hardened from work. A saw blade could have slipped right over his grandfather's hands and come off dull. Eli's hands were small and tan, but they weren't nearly as leathered as his grandfather's. Eli missed him, missed the stories his grandfather told him, stories about Cherokee ghosts that haunted the woods near their home and stories about people who could turn into animals. Skin-walkers, his grandfather had called them. The Raven Mocker was certainly the most frightening spirit, but not all of them were bad.

"You don't think the stories Grandad used to tell are real?" Eli asked. He knew his father didn't believe the stories.

"I think if you believe them, then they're real. Every person gets to decide for himself. It's good to spend time thinking about them, though." He winked at Eli. "Just not too much. The same goes for spending time in nature. It's good to get out there, but you can't spend all your time in the forest, not these days at least. You know, when I was just a little older than you," his father said as he sat down next to the mower. "I hiked the Appalachian Trail. Your grandfather did it when he was young, too."

Eli had heard this story before. Both his father and grandfather had carved their names in the same tree.

"One day, when you're a little older, and I can convince your mother that you won't die," his father said, chuckling and turning a bolt on the mower, "you'll hike the AT as well. Carve your name below mine. Then there'll be three generations of Suttons on it and the trail will never forget the family that bested it. Now, hand me that wrench, will you?" He pointed next to Eli's feet, paused for a moment, and then raised his head. "Where are your shoes, son?"

Eli wiggled his toes inside his socks. "Mom told me to take them off before going in the house."

"Well, this is the garage. You're going to get grease and dirt all over your socks. Go put something on your feet," his father said.

In the kitchen, his mom chopped vegetables. "Are you cooking dinner already?" Eli asked.

"I'm making soup. It won't be ready for a few hours. Did you get something to eat?"

Eli nodded his head.

"More than trail mix and a banana?"

Eli returned his mom's smile. She knew him well.

"Chop these carrots up and I'll make you a sandwich," she said.

Eli sat at the table, poking the tuna sandwich his mother had just made. He picked at the crust a little and dropped some crumbs on the floor. Pepper licked them up. He took a bite. Chewing, he said, "What about the AT, mom?"

His mother chopped an onion. "The what?"

Eli rolled his eyes. She knew what he was talking about. "The Appalachian Trail."

"What about it?" she said, blinking tears back.

"Well, school will be out soon," Eli said, "and I think this summer I could hike it."

His mother dumped the onion in the pot. It sizzled and bits of steam curled into the air. "Whew, those onions always get my eyes," she said.

Eli took another bite of the sandwich. "I said, I think this summer would be a good summer to hike it."

His mother rinsed the cutting board and knife. "I don't know, Eli. It's such a long hike. It's quite a bit different from camping in the backyard."

Eli swallowed. "The backyard? Mom, I hike all the way to Round Knob almost every weekend."

"Round Knob is only ten miles from here, Eli. The Appalachian Trail is 1,500 miles long."

"Actually, it's 2,181," Eli muttered around another bite of sandwich.

"Not to mention that the road goes up Round Knob," his mom said. "Your father told me the Appalachian Trail is a very difficult hike through some very thick forest."

"I've hiked through the forest," Eli said. "Yesterday, I went almost all the way to the North Carolina border."

His mom set the knife down on the counter with a clang. "I told you not to go past the Knob, Eli. Just one more reason those little excursions aren't going to happen anymore."

Eli groaned.

"Maybe in a year or two, baby," his mom said, "but right now, you're too young. Now finish your sandwich and go help your father."

Eli, defeated, slipped from the chair and went into the garage. His father had taken apart the mower and there was confusion on his face.

"I don't get it," his father said. "One day it's working fine, the next it's not. Things can change unexpectedly, Eli." He stood, leaving the disassembled machine at his feet. "I need to go into town for some parts." He winked at Eli as if they shared a secret. "And maybe an ice cream. Sometimes the bad leads to good. How about it?"

It was a twenty minute drive into Greenville. The pickup pulled onto the highway and Eli watched the fields pass. Large plots of rolling fertile farmland stretched out on both sides of the road. He imagined the windows of the homes they passed to be like giant eyes that glared at him. In the distance, red barns housed horses, and grazing cattle went about their business.

Eli's father pointed at the cattle. "The land wasn't always like this, Eli. When your grandfather was young, Tennessee saw some bad years. During the 1930s most people out here still didn't have electricity, and they were only making about a hundred dollars a year. Can you imagine that?"

Eli had more money than that from working odd jobs, mowing lawns in the city and such.

"We lead soft lives now," his father continued, "but soft lives weren't always the norm. We come from a long line of Appalachian farmers. Your grandfather grew up in a very different way than you and me. He raised hogs, fattened them on corn he grew, grown from soil he knew. People were just trying to survive back then." The fields sped past them. "Fighting the land, hunger, malaria. We were lucky to be born after all that."

Most of the stories Eli had heard his grandfather tell were Cherokee myths, not about malaria.

His father looked over at him as they approached the Baptist Church. The parking lot was filled with cars, and old men and women dressed in their Sunday best were gathered around the building's entrance, shaking hands and hugging.

"What's first? The hardware store or ice cream?" his father asked. He smiled at Eli.

Eli glanced up just in time to see a long gray sedan pull on to the road. He was close enough to see the driver, a withered man wearing a suit and tie, his head turned in the opposite direction. "Dad!" Eli yelled.

His father's head snapped back to the road and his hands gripped the wheel. Suddenly, Eli heard a loud noise like a thousand birds squawking in unison. It rang in his ears, and he felt glass on his skin, though it wasn't painful. It felt like cool water. As it flowed around him, he looked through the shattered windshield and saw the branches swaying in the wind. He rocked with them, listening to their creaking as he let the water carry him into darkness.

2

Eli held his mother's hand as she cried. She wore a black dress and he wore a charcoal suit. He could feel the fabric rub against his bandages. The pickup had flipped on its side when it collided with the sedan. Eli's shoulder and ribs and face had bounced along the pavement through the open passenger window. The cuts itched more than they hurt. Eli held the real pain inside. His father was dead.

Eli had been wearing his seatbelt; his father had not. He'd flown through the windshield and died of blood loss before the ambulance arrived. As he lay in a coffin, his face, heavily coated in makeup to cover the wounds, looked plastic.

Eli remembered very little of the accident, only the sensation of drifting down a stream. His grandfather once told him that water—lakes and rivers—were doorways into another world: the spirit world, the afterlife. Eli wasn't sure, but the sensation he felt during the crash—it made him wonder. It was like a dam had broken and the water had spilled around him, quickly carrying him away. Once the initial rush had passed, he felt like he was floating on his back in a deep, calm river. How long he drifted, he couldn't remember. The space and time there felt different. It was filled with something Eli didn't have a name for. After that, he woke up in the hospital, his mother by his bed.

Just four days and an eternity later, Eli sat next to his mother as friends and family filed past, saying how sorry they were and offering to help in any way possible. Eli wasn't sure what they could do. Anything short of bringing back his father was useless.

The funeral took place in a small church and the graveside service was short. His mother sobbed the whole time. Eli gripped her hand and cried silent tears, tiny but unstoppable rivers that poured down his cheeks and over his lips before falling from his jaw and forming lakes on his shirt collar.

Those lakes and rivers evaporated during the weeks following the funeral, but their dry forms remained. Water changes the landscape, forming it, shaping it, sometimes carrying it away; tears do the same to the mind. Eli definitely felt different. He felt a pressure building up inside him as if a great tree grew in his chest, and if he stopped moving for too long, its roots would burst from his feet and push into the soil. They would dig deep, coil around rock, lock him in place forever. Eli felt the need to move.

So he ran. He ran through the woods behind his house, for miles, until his lungs felt like bursting. He ran until he felt he would fall over, and then he would reach up and touch the healing scratches on his face, the place where his skin had scraped against the asphalt, and he would run some more.

He'd always preferred the outdoors, but after the accident, Eli found being inside almost unendurable. If he kept moving, he might be able to stop the roots from bursting through his feet, but he had no way to stop the budding branches growing in his mind. His thoughts needed room to grow.

The bright red scratches on his face turned brown and then pink. A few weeks after the funeral, near the end of May, Eli's mom brought a box into the kitchen and set it on the table. "These are some of your father's things," she said. "Things I think you should have." A few fat tears rolled from her eyes.

Eli peeked into the box. He recognized several of the items: a fly tying kit, a black-handled pocketknife, a red silk handkerchief with horses printed on it, a pack of cards, a few books, a handful of photos. But there was also something he hadn't seen before: an old leather-bound journal. Eli picked it up. Its cover was well-worn, the edges and corners a bit tattered, and it had a small flap with a button on it extending from the back cover to the front, keeping it closed. Eli unbuttoned the flap and opened it. The yellowing pages were filled with handwriting. He opened it to the first page. On the inside cover the words "Property of" were printed in fading black ink. Below this, there was a line, also printed in black ink, on which the handwritten name of Eli's grandfather appeared: Jack Sutton.

Eli's mom put a hand on his shoulder. "After your grandfather died, your father found that journal in his bedroom. I think he wrote most of it when he was in his teens. It's amazing it survived this long." His mother paused and then said, "I think I'm going to lie down for a bit."

Eli watched her walk into the back of the house. Pepper sullenly, obediently followed her. Eli reached for the journal. He flipped it open and read the first entry.

August 1st, 1933

Today is my birthday, and Mother gave me this journal. She bought it with some of the money my brother, Robert, makes working for the Civilian Conservation Corps, which Dad says is part of the president's New Deal. I'm not sure what kind of deal it is or what we get outside of twenty-five of the thirty dollars Robert makes a month working for the CCC. The other day, Mother read us a letter Robert wrote. In it, he said he's helping rebuild the country. He also said he's gained two pounds since he joined the CCC, says they're fattening him like a hog.

I wish I could go work with Robert, but Mother says I'm not old enough. I feel old enough, though. After all, it's been more than four years since all the banks flopped and more than three since Dad said we had to leave Knoxville and move to Grandad's farm. I've gotten used to it here, though. It's different than our life in Knoxville was. Not worse, just different.

Grandad's land is about 120 acres. He farms the north field, which is about 80 acres, and he leases out the south field. We live in the Big House. That's what everyone calls Grandad's house. Though, it's not all that big. There are a couple of other houses in the south field, the bunkhouses. That's where the tenant farmers live.

Eli skimmed the rest of the page. His grandfather's handwriting was tiny. The letters looped and swirled on top of each other. It was very different than Eli's writing, which was blocky and bulky. He flipped to the end of the journal.

Late July, perhaps

I'm at my trail's end. The earth is different up here. From the flat rock ledge where I'm sitting looking out across the landscape, the world is beautiful. To the west, a large valley and mountain. To the north, cliffs. To the east, rolling blue ridges surrounding several valleys filled with thick forest and lush grass, filled with life.

I feel my life will never be the same after this, but it's time I returned home. I carved my name in a tree just south of the ledge. Maybe one day I'll come back here and see how I've grown.

Eli knew his grandfather must have been talking about the tree his father told him about, the tree his father also carved his name in, the tree he would carve his name in. It was on Mount Katahdin, in Maine, at the end of the Appalachian Trail. He closed the journal, secured the button on the cover, and wrapped the silk handkerchief around it. He took the pocketknife out of the box. It had a sturdy black handle. The knife had belonged to his father and before that it belonged to his grandfather. For all Eli knew, it was the same knife both of them used to carve their names in that tree. He opened the blade. There were a few spots of rust on it, but the edge was in good condition. He closed it and slipped it in his jeans. It added weight to his pocket.

That night, he lay awake and read his grandfather's journal. He read the entire thing and then reread passages that stood out among the others, passages that spoke to him, passages that guided him.

He pictured his grandfather on the Appalachian Trail, writing in the journal, carrying the black-handled pocketknife with him. Eli pictured his grandfather's feet pressing into the dirt, leaving tracks that were swept away by rain. It's possible, even probable, that the tracks Eli's grandfather left on the AT were recreated forty years later in the same spots by Eli's father. And it was possible that Eli could recreate those same tracks again. He could walk in his father's and grandfather's footsteps. With this image in his mind, Eli drifted into the darkness of sleep.

The following day, Eli counted his money. If he was very frugal, he would have enough to hike the AT all the way to Maine. That night, he went to bed early and set his watch for three in the morning.

The watch beeped under his covers. He silenced it and peeked out of his room. Down the hall, his mom's bedroom door was closed. While she slept, Eli packed his rucksack, an old pack that had belonged to his grandfather.

In his bedroom, with the light turned low, Eli stuffed a fleece, a rain jacket, a couple of shirts, a few pairs of socks and underwear, an extra pair of pants, and a few pairs of shorts into his pack. He grabbed his wrist rocket off his desk and tossed it in as well. Then he slipped out of his room, softly closing the door behind him. His socked feet slipped along the hardwood.

He snuck into the garage. Blue-gray moonlight dimly lit the floor. He set his pack down and let his eyes adjust to the dark. He walked over to a shelf in one corner where the camping gear was kept. He felt his way along the shelf until he found a plastic box. He opened it and let his fingers fumble inside until they touched what he needed: a headlamp. He pulled it on and flipped the switch on the side. A beam of yellow light filled the box. He took a flashlight, his canteen, and his father's canteen and put them in his pack. He grabbed his sleeping bag and his solo tent from one shelf. He packed a compass, his camping shovel, a pot, a tin bowl and spoon, a can opener, and a first aid kit—all stuff he usually took with him on overnight trips. He would be out there much longer than one night, though. From another shelf he grabbed two lighters and a newspaper and stuffed them in his bag. He tried to think of what else he might need. He packed some extra batteries and a roll of duct tape, just in case.

Eli snuck back into the house, into the bathroom. He grabbed several rolls of toilet paper, his toothbrush, and toothpaste. Then he crept into the kitchen. He packed all the pasta in the cabinets, trail mix, boxed rice, oatmeal, dried fruit, two cans of stewed tomatoes, three cans of beans, two boxes of granola bars, a few cans of fruit, a jar of peanut butter, three apples, and two bananas. He took a box of sandwich bags and a box of garbage bags as well. He opened cabinets silently and slid the items into his bag. He lifted the pack a few times, feeling its weight. It was much heavier than he'd expected.

He went back into his room and packed the final item: his grandfather's journal, still wrapped in his father's silk handkerchief. He slid it into one of the sandwich bags and sealed it. He checked his pocket to make sure he had the black-handled knife, and he glanced at his watch. It was almost four in the morning. Despite only sleeping six hours, he was wide awake.

His heart pumped as he set his pack by the door and pulled a piece of paper from the printer. He wrote a short note to his mom explaining that he would be back in late September or early October and that she shouldn't worry about him. He knew she would. He had his phone with him, but he wouldn't turn it on unless there was an emergency. He didn't say where he was going.

Then he slipped away into the night, gently closing the screen door behind him. The air chilled his bare arms. At the end of the driveway, he took off his pack and put on his fleece. Hoisting the pack onto his shoulders again, he breathed deeply. He smelled the air and took a moment to admire the trees surrounding his house. Their branches reached toward the stars, holding the sky in place. His eyes trailed down their trunks and settled on his mom's bedroom window. It felt miles away already. "See you in four months," he said. His boots crunched on the gravel road.

Dee woke up around eight. She reached out and felt the sheets next to her. Sam was dead. She stared at the ceiling, feeling like she was sinking into the mattress. This happened every day. Her sleeping mind forgot each night, and her waking mind had to learn each morning. The information took time to rise to the surface, and when it did, it came in waves.

Tears poured from her eyes and slipped down her temples, wetting her hair and soaking into the pillow. She cried her morning tears and then dried her eyes with the sheet. After a moment, she went into the bathroom and blew her nose. She splashed some water on her face and looked in the mirror. Her eyes were red and sunken. They had been for the last month. She hadn't been eating, hadn't been taking care of herself at all, really. She probably would have stopped altogether if it wasn't for Eli. But for him, she had to keep going. Without Sam, they only had each other.

She reached for her toothbrush, but her hand stopped halfway. It was alone in the holder. Eli's toothbrush was gone. She opened the medicine cabinet. It wasn't there either, and the toothpaste was also missing.

"Eli?" she said as she walked down the hall to his room. "Eli, baby, you want some breakfast?" She knocked on his door. When no answer came, she opened it. His bed was empty. "Eli," she called again, louder, as she walked into the kitchen.

She glanced around the room and then saw the note. It was on the table underneath a salt shaker. Dee picked it up.

Her eyes buzzed over the page. Each word pulled a tear onto her cheek. She put the note on the table, picked up the phone, and called Ben Nelson, the county sheriff.

3

By eight in the morning, Eli crested Round Knob. He was walking southeast toward the Tennessee-North Carolina border. He stopped, peeled a banana for breakfast, and took in the view. Several ridges receded into the distance, turning from tan to brown to blue to gray as they got farther away. The path that led from Round Knob to the Appalachian Trail was only a couple more miles. After that, Eli would get on the AT, which ran almost directly in line with the border, zigzagging in and out of both states. Eli finished the first banana and started in on the second.

An hour and a half later, he saw the first white blaze of his journey: a white rectangle about six inches tall and two inches wide painted on a tree. The blazes marked the AT, guiding hikers through the forest. The side trails were marked with blue rectangles so hikers venturing off the path for water or to take in scenery didn't get lost in the woods.

Eli dropped his pack. He was in good shape, but nearly six hours of hiking was a lot. He stretched his legs. His thighs burned a bit, but it felt good. He planned to hike from morning until night, figuring he could cover twenty or thirty miles a day, depending on how steep the terrain was.

He studied the white blaze. He put his hand over it. The bark pressed into his palm. He traced it with his finger. He imagined his father and grandfather passing that blaze, looking at it, perhaps even stopping to eat lunch there. Eli took another deep breath and let his fingers slide down the tree trunk. He glanced back toward Round Knob. The forest blocked his view, but he knew what was back there. He knew his mom and home were back there, and he knew they still would be in four months. What he didn't know was what lay ahead of him. Images of birds and squirrels, trees and soil, mountains and earth flickered through his mind. A tiny string pulled him back toward his mom and home, but a thick rope, a rope as wide as the path, pulled him forward. He shouldered his pack and took his first steps onto the Appalachian Trail.

Instead of feeling like the earth was pulling him down, he felt like it was pushing him up. On this trail, he could hike for days without stopping. A smile spread over his face.

Ben Nelson and his deputy sheriff, Daryl Wright, pulled up in front of Dee's house. Before he was even out of his car, Dee rushed him and thrust a paper in his face. She was in a panic.

"Calm down, Dee," Ben said, taking the note from her hands.

"I think he's heading for the Appalachian Trail," Dee said. "I didn't know what to do. Should I have gone looking for him myself? I should have gone looking myself." She pushed tears from her eyes.

"You did the right thing callin' us, ma'am," Daryl said.

Ben crinkled his brow at him. Daryl shuffled his feet. Ben turned back to Dee. "You don't know how long he's been gone, so I'd say you made the right choice by not following him into the woods. One person can only search so far." Ben looked into the trees. They were thick with brush. "Why do you think he's headin' for the Appalachian Trail?"

"He's been wanting to hike it for a while. His father—" Dee burst into tears. She couldn't finish.

Ben sucked in a silent breath. Dee's boy had only been gone a few hours. He wasn't technically missing yet. But Ben couldn't tell Dee he wasn't going to look for her boy, not after she'd lost her husband just a month before. "I doubt he'll make the Appalachian Trail. It's a pretty good hike from here. Most likely he's just wandering around between here and Round Knob. Daryl and I'll take the cruiser up and see if we can spot him on the road up there."

Dee shook her head. "Eli hikes back there all the time. He's good out there in the woods."

Ben scratched his chin. It was miles to Round Knob and farther to the AT. Even if the kid knew the trails, he was still on foot. He couldn't have made it far.

Eli came to a stone shelter in a small clearing. The shelter had a rusting tin roof and three walls, one supporting a chimney. There was a picnic table and two tree trunks used as benches in front of a fire pit. The shelter was empty. A wood sign with yellow letters read "JERRY'S CABIN." It also said it was 5.9 miles to Flint Mountain Shelter and 13.9 miles to Hogback Ridge Shelter.

Eli glanced at his watch. It was almost eleven o'clock. Lunch time. He put his pack on the ground next to the picnic table. He opened a granola bar and used it to scoop peanut butter from the jar. As he ate the sticky paste, he stuck his head inside the shelter. It smelled a bit funky, like damp leaves, and though he didn't intend to sleep there, as he still had several hours to go before dark, he knew the AT was littered with similar shelters. He figured spending nights in them would save him time, as he wouldn't have to set up and tear down his tent.

He finished the granola bar and capped the peanut butter. His shoulders were getting a little sore and his calves were tight, but the string he felt tugging him back home when he first reached the AT had broken. All he felt was a tremendous drive to keep moving forward, and the white blazes called him back to the trail.

After a few miles, Eli had to relieve himself. He took his pack with him and hiked off the trail about fifty yards. He dug a small hole with the collapsible camping shovel and squatted. Pooping in the woods always made Eli feel a little vulnerable, which, he supposed, he was.

A little while later, he stopped in a clearing to remove his fleece. Sweat soaked his armpits and chest. As he tossed it in his pack, a titmouse sang in the trees behind him, and he almost sang back. Then he was off again, walking toward Big Butt Mountain.

He hiked along a ridge that contained several ups and downs, which burned his thighs, and he topped Big Butt Mountain mid-afternoon. The sky hugged green hills and a few low clouds drifted in the blue. On his descent, he saw a sign notifying hikers of bears in the area. He looked into the woods. Thin trees reached tall and a sea of bushes covered the forest floor, but Eli saw no bears. He figured as long as he was on the trail, he would probably be safe.

He continued on until he came to a meadow with three headstones. Eli glanced around the woods. It wasn't a graveyard. The headstones looked out of place. Eli walked over to them. One read "David Shelton," one "Wm. Shelton," and another "Millard F. Haire." Eli vaguely recalled his history teacher telling the class about David and William Shelton. They were killed by Confederates in the Civil War for fighting for the Union. Between the graves, planted flowers grew. Someone must have come up there and maintained them fairly often. Suddenly, Eli felt a little frightened. The grass and trees were still. Not a single bird sang. He continued walking. The rope pulling him forward, though, felt slightly slack.

The first people he saw were at Flint Mountain Shelter. He was tired and would have stopped hiking had the shelter been empty. It was much nicer than Jerry's Cabin and was made of logs, not stone. Six backpacks leaned against one of the shelter's walls, and several items of clothing hung from a rope strung between two trees. Four people were lying in the shelter, their bare feet hanging off the edge of the elevated sleeping area, and a woman and a man cooked something over a crackling fire.

The woman smiled as Eli approached the shelter. "Hey, little man." The man looked up from the flames and smiled as well.

Eli waved and walked past them, smelling the smoke. Behind him, he heard the man ask the woman, "Do you think he's hiking alone?" Eli's heart pounded and he quickened his pace. He didn't want to have to explain to anyone that he was out there against his mom's will. Though the idea was present prior to that moment, the vocabulary hadn't risen to the surface of his mind until then: he was a runaway. The word hugged his tongue as he hiked.

His legs really began to burn as the late afternoon sun flickered through the trees, lower and lower with each passing mile. He crossed several streams, all of which had footbridges built over them, and he climbed a steep incline he felt would never end; the trail just kept going up and up. In the distant woods he saw an old barn crumbling with age, a relic of farming times forgotten. He was tempted to stop hiking and sleep there. The pull he'd felt from the trail in the morning had subsided and the pep in his step was fading. He was tired and drenched in sweat. But he figured he must be getting close to the next shelter.

As he crested the mountain and began his descent, his step quickened and the white blazes flowed by, one after the other, on trees and on rocks, guiding him along as the shadows grew long. Soon, the sun would be gone.

Eli reached the bottom of the gap and stopped. The trail, littered with roots and rocks, turned up again. He licked his lips. His tongue was dry, his skin sticky with sweat. He was too tired to push through another climb, and he felt hungry. It was a different kind of hunger. It pulsated below his skin, quivering in his muscles, buzzing in his blood. He set down his pack and took out his canteen. Off the trail, grass carpeted the forest and tiny yellow flowers enticed the bees and insects.

Just as he was about to walk into the woods to set up camp, two hikers came toward him from the north. One of them was about Eli's age and the other was older. Their features were similar. Eli supposed they were father and son.

In between gulps of water, Eli asked, "Do you know how far it is to the next shelter?"

"Oh, about a mile," the older man replied.

Eli thanked him and picked up his pack.

The man hesitated. "You hiking alone?"

Eli's tongue reached for words. "No, I'm—I'm just a bit ahead of the pack," he said, nodding toward the trail behind him, as if any minute a large group of people would come down the hill.

The man laughed. "In better shape than the rest of the gang, huh? Well, good luck."

Eli thanked the man again and began ascending the next hill as the sun faded into twilight. Half an hour later, he found the shelter and was thankful it was empty. It was similar to the last one he passed, with an elevated sleeping area and a fire pit outside the entrance. Two signs were nailed on the wall. One pointed left and read "WATER," the other pointed right and read "PRIVY."

Eli dumped his pack inside, put on his headlamp, and tore open one of the granola bars. At the sight of food, the buzzing hunger left his blood and muscles and flowed into his stomach, where it groaned. He ate the granola bar in two bites and then dug out one of the cans of beans, which he ate cold. Then he ate an apple slathered in peanut butter and another granola bar. He fell back against his pack, the food heavy in his belly.

He glanced at his watch. It was almost eight o'clock. He'd walked a lot of miles that day. The next day would be lighter, the same pace but fewer hours hiking, as he wouldn't be waking up at three in the morning. He closed his eyes, and sleep, a dark carnivorous beast, began to eat his thoughts. He sat up before they were devoured entirely. He had one more thing to take care of before he could sleep: water.

He collected some dry twigs and leaves and started a fire using the newspaper and lighter. He fanned the flame and tossed in a few more sticks as it grew. Then he followed the blue blazes pointing in the direction of water. The woods spread out on both sides of him. It wasn't fully dark yet, but his headlamp was necessary. It was a longer hike than he expected. At the end of it, he found a small stream. The cool water flowed over his hands as he dipped his pot. Then he started back to the shelter.

Halfway back, he heard a rustling in the woods to his right. He turned, careful not to spill the water. The beam from his headlamp lit up the trees and cast long shadows into the woods. He waited a minute longer, straining to see what was out there, but he heard nothing more. He quickened his pace back to the shelter.

As he waited for the water to boil, he studied the flames. They fought with each other, competing for space on the wood, struggling just to breathe. The whole world was like that sometimes. All elbows and knees, shoving and shouting—a struggle just to breathe. But it was different in the woods. Things were simple there. His goals were simple.

Eli let the water boil for several minutes before removing it from the flame. When it was cooler, he would refill his canteens.

He set the alarm on his watch for six o'clock in the morning. If he intended to make Mount Katahdin by October, he needed to keep a pretty tight schedule. He pulled his sleeping bag from his pack and laid it on the wood as the crickets chirped behind him. Then he removed his boots and socks and pulled off his shirt. He spread the damp clothes on the picnic table outside the shelter to dry for the night. The sound of the crickets grew louder as the stars grew brighter. Eli smiled at the sky and felt the air on his back and arms. He touched the pink scars on his ribs and shoulder and then ducked back inside the shelter.

His salty skin rubbed against the bag as he snuggled inside. His father would have been proud of him. He felt the knife in his pocket. He reached over and removed his grandfather's journal from his pack. He pulled it from the plastic bag, unwrapped it from the silk handkerchief, and read the last entry again.

Late July, perhaps

*I'm at my trail's end. The earth is different up here. From
the flat rock ledge where I'm sitting looking out across the
landscape, the world is beautiful. To the west, a large valley and
mountain. To the north, cliffs. To the east, rolling blue ridges
surrounding several valleys filled with thick forest and lush
grass, filled with life.*

*I feel my life will never be the same after this, but it's time
I returned home. I carved my name in a tree just south of
the ledge. Maybe one day I'll come back here and see how I've
grown.*

Eli read those two paragraphs half a dozen times. His goal
was right there on the page. That tree was out there, and he
would find it.

Though he'd read the entire journal before leaving, he
flipped back to an earlier entry and reread it.

August 14th, 1933

*Dad talked about the stock market the other day. He said we're
in a depression. It's the reason we had to move. I remember the*

morning everything changed. Dad rushed to the bank. When he came back, he and Mother sat down at the kitchen table. I was in the living room. I watched them. Dad told Mother that our money was all gone, our life savings was all gone. I'm not sure how much money we had before 1929, but I know how much we had after. None! We spent a few more months in Knoxville after that. Dad looked for work. But it wasn't long before we packed up everything and drove to Grandad's place. Sometimes I still miss our place in Knoxville. It was smaller than Grandad's farm, sure, but my brother and I had less work to do.

Dad worked in a factory there, but before I was born he was an ambulance driver in the war. He married Mother as soon as he got home. He said he didn't want her to live on Grandad's farm. He said there was more money and a better life for us in Knoxville. He said no one in Coal Creek had money.

Grandad's farm is about thirty miles from Knoxville.

We'd drive out here once a month or so during the summer and sometimes for holidays, but we never stayed too long. The house seemed so different than our place in Knoxville. It seemed about to fall over, if only one good wind would have blown at it. I know better now, though. It's real sturdy.

I remember the day we moved here for good. Grandad greeted us and invited us in. Dad told Grandad all about what was going on in Knoxville, about the banks closing, the soup lines opening, the men and women and families sleeping on the streets. Grandad listened, nodding his head and scratching his chin. When Dad stopped talking, Grandad walked over to a cabinet in the living room and took out a tin can. He shook the can at my dad and the rattling of coins jingled through the house. He said that's why you don't keep your money in a bank. You keep it safe at home.

I think Robert didn't like living on the farm. He was always a little angry when he was here compared to when we lived in Knoxville. Grandad works us hard. Maybe that's what Robert didn't like, or maybe he just didn't like the change. I hope he's happier working with the CCC.

I don't mind it here. In Knoxville all Mother cooked was soup and biscuits. The soup was always thin and the biscuits always hard. Here at Grandad's, though, we eat meat. Grandad has pigs, and we always have plenty of vegetables. Grandad grows corn and squash and okra, and some tobacco, though he sells that.

Also, out here I can hunt jackrabbits. Now that Robert's gone, I hunt alone, but we used to go out together and pick off four or five of them in an hour. Mother skins them and makes soup. The days are longer here than in Knoxville, though. I get up when Dad gets up, and he always wakes with the sun. In the winter I go to school during the day, except sometimes when it's harvest season and Grandad's shorthanded. But after school, instead of playing with Robert like I did in Knoxville, I work, sometimes until dark spills over the fields. Then I run back to the house for supper. I run so that U`tlun'ta doesn't get me.

I'd never tell anyone this, but U`tlun'ta terrifies me. Mother tells me stories about Cherokee Indians that lived in the Appalachian Mountains before the Europeans arrived. She also tells me stories about spirits that inhabit the woods and rivers. Many of them can only be seen by strong medicine men. U`tlun'ta is a bad one.

According to Mother, U`tlun'ta is a witch covered in rock-like skin that breaks anything you shoot at it, and her right forefinger is long and sharp as a spear. That's why she is named U`tlun'ta; it means "spear-finger." Mother says U`tlun'ta lives in the mountains and hunts children. She calls to them, lures them into her lap, and when they fall asleep, she stabs them through the heart with her long finger and eats their livers. She prowls the Appalachian forests, looking for people walking alone. She hunts them, stalks them like I stalk rabbits, and she can take the form of anyone she likes. It's safer to travel in groups because of U`tlun'ta, because if someone goes out to hunt or fetch water alone, the group can never be sure if it's U`tlun'ta returning, disguising herself as the hunter.

I doubt she's real, but when I walk alone on Grandad's land, I can't help but look at the shadows and think she might be lurking among them. I hope I never see her. Sometimes, when I'm in the fields near the woods, I think I hear her calling me. That's when I put my hands over my ears and run.

U`tlun'ta isn't the worst of the spirits, though. Mother says the Raven Mocker is the worst and strongest. Even

U' tlun'ta is afraid of him. He often disguises himself as an old person and hunts sick and dying people. By feeding on the hearts of his prey, the Raven Mocker can extend his own life. If the Raven Mocker eats the heart of a man who has six months to live, then the Raven Mocker gains six months more to live. The Raven Mocker can soar through the air like a bird, too. Sometimes, I lie awake at night, fearing that if I fall asleep the Raven Mocker will fly down from the sky and land on my chest and devour my heart.

Not all the spirits Mother tells me about are evil. The Little People called the Yunwi Tsunsdi are my favorite. They are, supposedly, about two feet tall and have long hair. They live in the mountains near here, Mother says, and they often help people who are lost or sick. Sometimes, if you listen very hard, she says, you can hear them singing and drumming.

Eli's eyes closed and the journal slipped from his hands. Sleep overcame him, silently and completely. He dreamt his father and grandfather were still alive, but they weren't living in his time. Instead, Eli and his father were living on a farm with his grandfather in 1933. Eli worked next to his grandfather in a field. Both of them were fourteen years old.

The dream faded into the beeping of his wrist watch. By the time Eli turned off the alarm, the dream had receded entirely, going back to the land where dreams roam free, unconstrained by the mind. Eli lay in the bag for a minute longer, tempted to sleep another hour. But then he heard a muffled scratching. He sat up, listening. The wind blew through the trees above the shelter. Eli looked out the entrance and the woods glared back. It was still dark, but he knew the sun would crest the horizon soon. Then Eli heard it again. Scratching and gnawing. His heart jumped. Something was just outside the shelter. His ears strained to hear. Seconds passed. Then he heard it again. It wasn't outside the shelter. It was in there with him.

№ 4

Ben Nelson sat at his desk, his uniform loosened at the collar. His fingers pecked away at the keyboard. They'd searched the woods between Dee's home and Round Knob all day and into the night and hadn't found Eli. It was time to put the call out. He was writing an email to the Forest Service, asking them for help locating Eli. If he was on the Appalachian Trail, the rangers should easily find him. Ben was also sending the email to the surrounding county sheriffs and the city police, just in case Dee was wrong about where Eli was going.

He pressed send and rolled his neck. It was early morning. Daryl had gone home before midnight the previous night. Ben had fallen asleep on the couch in his office.

He felt sorry for Dee. First she'd lost her husband in a car accident, and then her boy had run away. Life was cruel sometimes. Ben was confident they'd have him back soon, though. He put on his hat and headed home. Daryl would be in to open up shop before long. Ben was going to go catch a few hours of sleep and take a shower.

Eli grabbed his headlamp and flipped it on. The shadows disappeared. Nothing was in the shelter with him, but the scratching sound continued. He turned. It was coming from his pack.

He slowly slipped from his sleeping bag. The cool air gripped his bare skin. He reached toward his pack, still hearing the sounds of scratching, and flung open the flap.

Mice rushed out, four or five of them. They scattered in all directions, and Eli fell onto his back. One ran directly up his leg, jumped onto his sleeping bag, and darted out of the shelter.

Eli lay on the sleeping bag, catching his breath and recuperating from the scare. After a minute he poked his pack, making sure no mice remained inside it. Then he dumped the contents onto the shelter floor. They'd chewed through the box of granola bars and several of the wrappers, and the third apple had teeth marks all over it—mice. Damn mice.

He unwrapped the chewed-on granola bars and threw them and the apple into the woods. Then he ate the untouched bars and a can of fruit. Eli had camped dozens of times in the woods and not once had mice bothered him. He supposed the AT shelters were frequented by more people than the woods near his home. People meant food and food meant rodents. From then on he would have to hang his pack from a tree branch or from the rafters of the shelter while he slept.

He brushed his teeth and pulled on his shirt. He stretched. His skin felt tight, his legs a little sore, and a pinch spread from his neck down his back. He wasn't used to carrying such a heavy pack. But he supposed he would get used to it in the coming weeks.

Eli repacked his bag. He pulled on the same socks he wore the first day and laced his boots. He took a deep breath as he lifted his pack onto his shoulders. It seemed to weigh twice as much as it did the day before.

Less than an hour into the day, the trail turned up a steep incline, another one that seemed to never end. Eli grimaced as he climbed. The ups seemed steeper and the downs seemed flatter, as if the world had tilted a few degrees, just enough to give him a little more of a challenge. The salt from the previous day's sweat rubbed between his legs. It wasn't long before the chaffing became unbearable and Eli had to stop walking.

He sat down on a large rock just off the trail and let the pack slip to the ground. It landed in the dirt and grass with a clank and a thud. He rolled his shoulders. The pinching pain had turned to a steady ache. It radiated across his back in waves, one after the other. He could manage with that pain. The chaffing on his legs was another story. He unzipped his pants and pulled them down. The inside of his thighs were rubbed red. Touching the rash sent a sting through his skin.

He pulled his pack a little farther off the trail, just out of sight if anyone walked by. He sat on a fallen tree and took off his shoes, followed by his pants, which he rolled up and tossed into his bag. Then he removed his sweat-stained underwear. He scrunched his face as he wadded them into a ball and shoved them in his pack.

He poured some water from his canteen over the rash. It stung, but also felt good, flowing down his legs and cooling the red skin. As the water dried, he dug through his first aid kit. It contained an assortment of medicine, bandages, tweezers, and tape. Eli took out a tube of A+D ointment and squeezed a large bit of it onto his fingers. He rubbed it into the rash. The pain was followed by a soothing sensation.

He put the ointment and first aid kit back in his pack and took out his shorts. They fit a bit looser than his pants. He pulled them on and then shoved his feet back into his boots. He stood up and took a few steps. The rash still burned, but it was much better than before. He could actually walk without grimacing

He ate a few handfuls of trail mix and pressed on, thinking about his grandfather and the stories he'd told. He wished he could go back in time and listen to them again. But at least he had the journal and he could read his grandfather's words. Like his grandfather, Eli enjoyed the stories about the Little People of the forest, the Yunwi Tsunsdi, best. Eli knew the stories weren't real, but that didn't stop him from liking them—imagining them living in the forest, chattering to each other, singing, dancing. He wished that he would look into the woods and see them. They were supposedly very helpful. His grandfather had told him stories about the Yunwi Tsunsdi finding lost children and bringing them back to their parents. They even sometimes, supposedly, helped harvest the corn. Eli wondered what he would say to them if he met them. Would he greet them? Would he pretend he hadn't seen them? The Yunwi Tsunsdi—the Little People of the forest.

Suddenly, Eli realized he hadn't seen a white blaze in quite some time. He'd been lost in thought. He surveyed the trees around him—nothing. He scanned the rocks— nothing. He walked a few more yards and still saw no blazes. They marked the trail in fairly regular intervals, intervals that were pretty short. He walked another thirty yards or so and still saw nothing. He spun in a circle, scanning each tree and every rock. There was no sign of the trail. In all directions, the woods were the same: a wall of birch and maple trees held together with ferns and moss.

Ben sipped his coffee as he climbed out of his cruiser. He hadn't been able to sleep, but the shower had felt good. Putting on a fresh crisp uniform felt good.

Daryl glanced up from his desk as Ben entered. "Mornin', boss. Someone called for you earlier."

Ben waited for Daryl to finish, but Daryl just looked at him. After a few seconds, Ben rolled his eyes and said, "Who was it, Daryl?"

"Oh, sorry. Um, I wrote down her name." Daryl searched his mess of a desk. Crumpled papers and candy wrappers covered it.

Ben pinched the bridge of his nose. "Just tell me what she said, Daryl."

"It was a forest ranger. She said she got your email and they would be looking for Eli on the AT, starting at ..." Daryl grabbed a sticky note from under a fast food wrapper. "Found it! They started near Interstate 26 and are heading south. She said there's no way he could have gotten farther than that in a single day."

Ben sipped his coffee. "Good," he said as he walked toward his office. He paused halfway down the hall. "And clean your damn desk, Daryl. It's a disgrace."

In his office, Ben dialed Dee's number and told her about the rangers searching for her son. "We'll have him home soon," he said before hanging up.

Eli knew which direction he'd come from. Or at least he thought he did. He tried to retrace his steps. He inspected the ground, watching for any sign of human passage, and he surveyed the trees, waiting to see a white blaze. After five minutes he was worried. After ten he was panicked. He told himself to remain calm, to focus.

He did neither. He rushed through the brush. It was only his second day on the trail and he was already lost, already failing. Sweat poured down his face. His thighs burned and his shoulders hurt. Mosquitoes landed on his neck and he swatted them away. He pushed his hair off his wet forehead and stopped. What would his father do? What would his grandfather do?

He closed his eyes and recalled the last white blaze he'd seen. Was it on a rock? A tree? Yes, it was on a rock. He had stepped directly on it. That was about—he let the world soak into his mind, tried to feel the time swirl around him—that was about half an hour before, maybe. That was about right. Not too much time had passed. He pictured the sun overhead. When he stepped on that blaze, where had the sun been? He stared into the backs of his eyelids as if a movie projector replayed the morning's events on them. He couldn't remember seeing where the sun had been, but he did remember the shadows. They'd stretched out behind him, almost parallel with the trail. That couldn't be right, though. He opened his eyes.

He was hiking the trail south to north. He dropped his pack and took out his compass. He faced north. The mid-morning shadows stretched to his left, so they should have hit the trail almost perpendicularly. But the trail followed the border and the border wasn't a straight line, so of course the trail changed directions periodically.

He closed his eyes again. The compass pressed on his hand. The air dripped with sweat. He focused on the rock with the white blaze. He saw his foot cover the blaze. He saw the shadows of the trees. They were coming toward him almost directly. That meant he'd been walking east almost directly.

He opened his eyes. The compass looked up at him. He turned until its needle pointed east, and he started walking. He didn't know if he'd veered off the path to the north or to the south. All he knew was that he'd been walking east the last time he was on the trail. Maybe if he continued walking east, the AT would veer back through his path.

He walked through the brush, still scanning each tree for a white blaze, checking each rock for the mark. He gulped water from his canteen and swatted mosquitoes from his face. Being off the trail and guideless made the woods a strange place. It was different than the forest around his home. Eli knew each and every tree in those woods, for miles and miles. He knew their branches, their bark, their knots, and their roots. In unfamiliar woods, though, the trees seemed indistinguishable from each other.

Eli stopped walking. To his left, the trees cleared. Dragonflies drifted around yellow flowers, flowers whose stems flexed in the breeze, whose leaves captured the sun. Under the flowers, the body of a rodent buzzed with flies.

"I'm going to die out here," Eli said. The sound of his voice was dissonant among the trees. "I'm going to die in strange woods." He glanced around. The trees seemed to bore down on him. "Are you ignoring me?" he said, raising his voice. It carried into the distance. "I know your friends," he said. "Quite well, actually." The woods didn't reply. "You're just going to let me wander?" He took a few more steps and then stopped again. "This really isn't fair." His voice grew louder as his panicked heart pumped.

Still, the woods were silent. He walked a few more yards, mumbling under his breath, cursing the forest. Then he screamed, "You know my dad just died!" He slung his shoulders back, letting his pack slide off them. He grabbed a rock and threw it at a tree, but missed. It crashed into the brush and a bird flew out. It flapped hard and quick, up and up, then glided for a second, sank, and flapped some more. It disappeared into the trees.

Eli sat down cross-legged. He wiped sweat from his cheeks. His breathing slowed. Then he heard a low sound, a bit like a zipper closing. He knew what it was immediately. He grabbed his pack and ran forward.

In less than a minute, the forest dropped away and Eli looked down at a road. Trucks and cars zipped over it. He saw a sign that marked Interstate 26. Farther north, a smaller sign marked the Appalachian Trial. His fear and anger slipped away. He crept from the woods and almost fell down the steep embankment. He walked along the highway until he came to an overpass where the interstate crossed a road named Flag Pond, which led back to the Appalachian Trail.

Above him, the cars rumbled on the bridge. As he crossed Flag Pond, a man called to him from a parking area on the right side of the road. Eli's throat clenched and he kept walking, pretending not to hear him over the whine of trucks on the highway. About a hundred feet away, a white blaze marked a post.

The man called out to him again. "Hey, come here a second. I'm talking to you." He pointed at Eli.

Eli slowed his pace and shielded his eyes from the sun. The man waved him over, looking up and down the road to make sure no cars were coming. A few other people in the parking area turned toward Eli.

Eli glanced to his left. The AT was right there. He wasn't positive what the man wanted, but he guessed his mom had probably reported him missing. He figured he had two options. He could run up the AT and duck into the woods, but the man would probably catch him in a matter of seconds. Eli's pack weighed him down too much. His second option seemed his best bet.

Eli pointed at himself as if he was confused. The man nodded. Eli made a show of checking the road, making sure it was clear, and then he crossed. He wiped his forehead as he approached the man, whose shirt was soaked with sweat.

"What's your name?" the man asked, gulping water from a plastic bottle.

"Jack," Eli said. He didn't want to give the man his real name and his grandfather's name came to mind first.

"I was just finishing a morning hike when two forest rangers came through here asking if I'd seen a kid about your age named Eli." The man glanced up the road. "You hiking alone?"

"No," Eli said.

"Then who are you with?" The man gulped some more water and stretched his leg.

"My father and grandfather."

"Where are they?"

Eli swallowed. One moment his mouth was empty and the next it was filled with words. "My grandfather's got the squirts. My dad's waiting for him." Eli pointed behind him. "A few miles or so back. It was real bad. Crapped his pants. My dad said I could go on ahead as long as I stuck to the trail." The words seemed to slip from the empty air onto his tongue without his consent.

The man raised his lip. "Gross," he said.

"Yeah, it was real nasty." Eli heard himself laugh. "It happened right on the trail, too. It was all over his—"

"All right, all right," the man said, but he didn't seem entirely convinced. "How far back is your pop?"

"Like I said, a few miles or so. I'm just looking for a shady spot to stop and wait for them, off the road."

The man nodded. "If you and your pop and grandad come across a kid hiking alone, tell them to call the rangers. They're looking for him for some reason."

"Yes, sir."

"Go on," the man said, "get your shade. Don't hike off the path to find it, though. There are bears and all kinds of critters in those woods."

Eli turned and headed for the trail. The conversation made him feel like more than a runaway. He felt like a fugitive.

His boots began to wear on his heels. They dug deeper in with each step, but Eli pushed forward.

The next few miles of trail led past several homes. He walked through pastures fluttering with activity. Butterflies and bees, grass and flowers, pollen and life, it all drifted around him, surrounded him, held him as if he was a speck of dust in a giant cupped hand. He walked over the wrinkles and folds until he came to the base of a large peak. The trail sloped up through the forest and climbed over rocks. He swayed from side to side, testing his feet. He gripped the straps on his shoulders. The pack pressed into his back, and he started the climb.

Before long, sweat dripped down his back and face, and he stopped to catch his breath near a sign pointing to a bypass and warning hikers to never cross summits during lightning storms. The sky was clear; only white wisps smeared the horizon, so Eli plodded on. The trail wasn't too rough, but because his feet hurt, it took him longer to climb than it should have.

At the summit, he stopped for lunch. As he opened a can of beans, he looked at the peaks below him. Other than a few drifting birds, the earth was motionless, still as a painting. The hills—waves of soil—washed in from the horizon. He finished the beans and opened a can of fruit. He turned north. Mount Katahdin was out there, and so was the tree with his father's name carved in it. He gulped down the fruit and put the can in his pack.

He descended the peak, following the trail onto a ridge of rock like a dinosaur's back, plated with stone and bone. The rock protruded from the path, and he almost fell twice, almost rolled his ankles on the jagged earth. He slowed his pace a bit, using more caution. An injury could end his journey.

The ridge gradually flattened and the forest folded over him. A string of silk snagged his face. He brushed it away. Above him, a web as big as him was lashed between two trees. A yellow and black spider hung in its center. As Eli passed, he imagined what it would be like to live the life of a spider, the acrobat of the insect world, balancing on thin wire, swinging like a trapeze artist high above the ground.

He was pulled from his imagination by a biting pain. It felt like a wasp or bee had stung him, and he almost swatted at his leg, but stopped. The skin of his right leg was covered in red bumps. It felt like it was on fire. He turned around. Among the thick growth was stinging nettle. He hadn't seen it. He'd been too far inside his head. He poured some water on the affected area. A thousand tiny pickaxes hammered his skin. He wanted to scream, in pain and in stupidity. It was not his day.

He rubbed some of the A+D ointment on it, but it didn't help. He recalled his father telling him that stinging nettle burns were caused by an acid and that you could treat them with baking soda. But he didn't have any baking soda.

By that afternoon, the burn had turned from needles dancing on his skin to a rubbing and rippling pain that swelled and retracted in his flesh. It swung like a pendulum and so did the trail. The path looped back and forth in long switchbacks, crossing several small ridges and streams. He stopped at one and let the water flow over the nettle burn, but it only provided temporary relief.

Not long after that, he reached a shelter. There was a plaque on it that read, "CHEROKEE NATIONAL FOREST," and above that, "NO BUSINESS SHELTER."

Eli flexed his leg and couldn't help but wonder: Did he have "no business" out there? He dropped his pack. He was done for the day.

Ben watched the clock. It was getting late and he still hadn't heard from the rangers. They should have already found Eli. "Daryl," he called down the hallway. No answer. Ben stood up and walked into the front office.

Daryl's eyes were closed, his mouth open, a tiny bit of drool dripped down his lip. Ben sighed. At least Daryl had cleaned his desk a little. He clapped next to Daryl's ear.

Daryl jumped. "Yes, sir," he said, and his hands automatically went to the keyboard and mouse as if he'd been working.

"Give that ranger a call back, the one you spoke with this morning," Ben said.

Daryl rubbed the sleep from his eyes.

"Are you listening, Daryl?"

"Yes, sir." He stopped touching his face and intently looked at Ben.

"Call the ranger and ask her how far they've searched."

Daryl picked up the phone, his finger hovering over the number pad. He set the phone back down and started shuffling through his papers.

"Lost the message again?" Ben asked.

Daryl nodded. "I'll find it. Don't worry." He stood up and started digging through the trash. "Ah! Here it is."

Ben rolled his eyes. "Give it to me." He snatched the note and went back to his office, where he plopped down and tried to read the note. It looked like it had been written by a gorilla playing with a pencil. "Daryl! Get back here and tell me what your damn handwriting says."

Daryl rushed down the hall and took the note from Ben. He read him the number and Ben dialed. Then Daryl leaned on the desk, staring at Ben. Ben waved him away like a fly.

The ranger put Ben on hold while she called the two rangers searching for Eli. Ben listened to the silence. A minute later, the phone clicked again.

"They're almost to Jerry's Cabin, near the side trail leading to Round Knob," she said. "If he was on the AT, they would have seen him by now."

"I was afraid of that," Ben said.

"Maybe he headed south?" she asked.

"Maybe. More likely his mother's wrong, and he's just wandering through the woods somewhere behind her house. We'll start searching for him again."

"Well, tomorrow I can send a couple rangers south on the trail, just to check."

"I'd appreciate it." Ben hung up the phone. He sighed and called Dee.

Eli made a fire in front of the shelter and then hiked back to the stream. He scooped some of the cool water onto his leg and his flesh bumped. He heard a twig snap. His head shot up and he scanned the trees. The swirling bark flowed from their branches, down the trunks, and spilled into the grass. Their roots snaked in and out of the dirt, gripping the earth as if something tugged at them from above. But nothing moved. Nothing was there. "Just the Yunwi Tsunsdi," Eli said and laughed. His voice sounded out of place, misplaced even, among the trees. He filled his pot with water and hiked back to the shelter.

While he waited for the water to boil, he took off his boots and examined his feet. On the back of both heels, large blisters had formed. Both had burst sometime during the day. The skin was loose and moist. He dug into his first aid kit and took out a tube of antibacterial cream. He squeezed a glob of it onto both blisters and covered them with Band-Aids. The first aid kit contained a bit of moleskin, as well. He would need to cut pieces of the soft, adhesive-backed fabric to protect his heels before starting in the morning.

He tossed the pasta into the water and read his grandfather's journal while it cooked.

September 2nd, 1933

I miss Robert a lot. We got another letter from him today. It was very hard for Dad to read it. I think he feels guilty for having told Robert to join the CCC, especially since Robert had to lie about being part Cherokee, or Ani-yun-wiya as Mother calls us. Either way, they have special camps, Dad says, for people with American Indian blood.

Robert said he's working on whatever projects the government deems necessary. How they choose, he didn't say. He did say he's mostly building bridges and roads, but that other CCC boys work with the land, planting trees to stop erosion and such. They're building flood controls and erecting fire lookout stations too. He says they've also been called out to fight a few fires. It sounds exciting.

Dad says Robert is making more money in a couple of months in the CCC than the farm makes in a year. He said they feed him and house him for free, too. I asked Mother again today if I could join the CCC. She said you have to be seventeen years old. Maybe in another couple of years I'll go work with Robert, but for now, I'm stuck here. It's not so bad, though. The school is in a cabin about a mile down the road. I'm the oldest boy that attends, and I have to share a room with the little ones, but Ms. Wilkerson is nice. She's been my teacher the whole time we've lived here.

Dad says school is important. Most of the kids go when they're little, but a lot of boys my age don't. They work instead. Dad says that I need to keep going unless I want to work the fields until I'm old. It wouldn't be so bad, though. It's hard work, but what work isn't? Dad says the land in the Tennessee Valley has been farmed too hard for too long, though. He says the soil here is worthless, and that the farm is hardly able to produce enough food to feed the family, much less enough to sell. He also says most of the country has electric lights and water that flows right from the wall. He says Tennessee is living in the Dark Ages, but I don't think it's so bad. I'm writing this by candlelight right now. It's not so dark.

Dad talks a lot about President Roosevelt. He says he's created something called the Tennessee Valley Authority that will help us. It's going to change the way we live.

Eli set the journal down and stirred the pasta. His grandfather lived in hard days.

As he drained the water and poured a can of tomatoes over it, an old man came up the trail. He had a large pack on and a hiking pole in each hand. He walked in a steady pace, not slowing a bit as he approached. Then he abruptly stopped. Without saying anything, he delicately leaned his poles against the shelter and slipped his pack from his shoulders. He propped it against the shelter as well, and then he walked around the wall and out of sight.

Eli wasn't sure what to do. It was almost as if the man hadn't even seen him. He took a bite of pasta. Should he pack his things and go? It would be full dark soon. He didn't want to have to set up his tent by flashlight.

A minute later, the man came back around the shelter and stood next to Eli. A long white mustache covered his lips and curled onto his cheeks. His chin protruded from his beard like a bald mountain surrounded by clouds. "Sorry about that," he said. "I didn't mean to be rude, but I really had to pee. My name's Hoary Jory." He held out a knobby hand that seemed to be more knuckles than fingers.

Eli shook it. "Your name is Hoary Jory?" he said.

"Well, my trail name is Hoary Jory," the old man said. "And you might be?" He theatrically waved his hand through the air.

"Jack," Eli said.

"Ah, and what's your trail name, Jack?"

Eli took another bite of pasta. "I guess I don't have one."

The old man's gray eyebrows rose and his forehead squished into wrinkles. "Don't have one? Well, that's too bad, Jack. A trail name is important. It's your identity in the woods—and to the woods." The old man smiled at the trees. "They don't recognize birth names."

"The trees?" Eli asked.

"That's right! You have to earn your name out here. For instance," the old man said, "my name was given to me by a fellow hiker. The Hoary is for," the old man twirled his white mustache around his fingers and then let it fall back in place, "well, I suppose that's obvious. And Jory is a nickname I've had since I was a kid." The old man glanced around and then whispered, "My real name's George, but don't tell them that." He pointed to the trees. "My feet are killing me. Would you mind if I joined you, Jack?"

Eli shook his head.

The old man brought his pack over and plopped down on the log across from Eli. "I'd also ask if I could borrow some of that fine flame you've got. Do you mind?"

"Go ahead," Eli said.

"Thank you," the man said. "Is that your pack in the shelter? What am I saying? There's only two of us here. Of course it's your pack. Silly me." He chuckled. "What I meant to say was, where did you get your pack?"

Eli's rucksack was made of olive green canvas. It was much simpler than the old man's pack, which had a frame built in and thick padding on the straps. "It was my grandfather's," Eli said.

"Well, it's certainly unique. Probably a bit painful on the shoulders, however. No?"

It was indeed. Eli's shoulders were rubbed red and raw. Eli only nodded.

You're a man of—" the old man eyed Eli and corrected, "a young man of few words. I, on the other hand, you will find, say a lot of words." The old man smiled. "Words, words, words."

Eli laughed, mostly out of discomfort.

"I also see that you've got quite a patch of nettle burn there." He pointed at Eli's leg. "I got into some a few years ago," he continued, removing a metal container from his pack. "It was all over my hands and arms. Terrible stinging rash." He held the container out to Eli. "I never hike without carrying a remedy for it now."

The fire reflected in the flat, silver container. The old man held it in the air between them.

"Don't trust me?" he said. A smile lifted his mustache. "Take it. It's my own concoction. Rub it on the burn."

Eli set down his pasta and took the container. He pulled off the lid. Inside was a sticky orange goop that smelled lemony. He scooped some out with two fingers and rubbed it on his leg. Instantly, the burning faded and his leg muscles relaxed. In fact, relieving the pain in his leg also seemed to give his whole body permission to relax.

"Better?" the old man—Hoary Jory—asked.

"So much," Eli said. "Thank you."

"You're welcome." Hoary Jory dumped a box of rice into a small camp pot and continued talking as he poured water over it. "You can never get too much trail magic, I say. The AT is abundant with it. Hikers help each other out here. People from all over offer you rides into towns, encourage you to keep going, even in small ways." He pushed the pot into the coals. "Where are you from?"

Eli looked up from the fire. "Tennessee," he said.

"Ah, a local. I see. How far are you hiking?"

Eli swallowed. "Maine."

"A thru-hiker. Very ambitious of you. I myself am only on the trail for four weeks. I attempted a thru-hike in the seventies, but I only made it to central Virginia." He pulled the pot a little farther from the flame. "Now, I'm going to assume there's a reason you're hiking alone, just as I have my reason for hiking alone, but I won't be so rude as to ask what your reason is." The man glanced at the journal next to Eli. Then his eyes drifted up and locked on Eli's.

Silence spread between them. It globbed onto everything, mucking up the air Eli breathed and making his food taste like mud. Eli didn't know why, but he felt he had to break the silence. "My dad just died."

Hoary Jory nodded. "I see. Well, I'm sorry to hear that. My spouse recently passed. Loss isn't easy."

Eli's attention drifted into the flames. His dad's death must have been hard for his mom. As his mind turned, the moment also turned. Eli could almost feel time rollover, as if he sat on a giant clock and the cranking of its insides vibrated his bones. The silence again stretched between Eli and Hoary Jory, but this time, Eli didn't know how to break it. He just ate his pasta.

Hoary Jory opened a can of peaches and stared into the fire. "How old are you?" he asked.

"Fourteen," Eli replied.

"Hiking all the way to Maine at fourteen—you're very brave," Hoary Jory said. His words settled from the air like dust, coating Eli's skin. Then he asked, "Are you familiar with the Cherokee?"

Eli said nothing. Suddenly, he felt like the old man knew more about him than he was letting on. Had he been following him? Had he crept into his shelter the night before and read his grandfather's journal? That was impossible, ridiculous even, but still, Eli's spine quivered.

"There's a legend about the Cherokee," the old man continued. "When a boy was about your age, maybe a little younger, his father would take him into the woods and blindfold him. Have you heard this story?"

Eli knew it. His grandfather had told it several times. He shook his head, though.

"Well, it's a very good story. I'll share it with you if you don't mind."

"Go ahead," Eli said.

"The father would tell his blindfolded son," Hoary Jory continued, "'If you want to be a man, you must do what I say. You must sit here on this stump all night long. And you mustn't take off the blindfold. No matter what you hear. No matter how bad your fear gets. You must not move from the stump, you must not sleep, and you must not remove the blindfold until the morning sun shines through it.' The boy, wanting to obey and impress his father, prove to him he was courageous, would of course agree. During the night the boy would sit on the stump. The wolves would howl in the distance. His imagination would run away with him as sleep and fear fought each other in his mind. He would hear giant serpents slithering through the grass when only a hare was there. He would feel the breath of a bear on his neck, when only the wind was blowing by.

"If the boy was courageous enough, he would last all night. And when the morning light pierced the blindfold, he would remove it, only to find that his father had been sitting next to him all night, ensuring that no harm came to him." Hoary Jory looked from the coals to Eli, the flames wiggling in his eyes. "Don't take the blindfold off until morning. Keep your pace steady and your mind free of fear. If you do that, you'll reach your goal."

Eli nodded his head and let his eyes fall back to the fire.

Hoary Jory pulled his rice from the coals. Then he repeated Eli's fake name. "Jack. No, that just won't do. If you're going to be out here among the woods and wild, you need something with a little more kick. A little more zam! You know what I mean?" Hoary Jory squinted at him. "Jack," he said. "Jack from Tennessee. Jack who's yet to remove his blindfold." Hoary Jory paused, then laughed and said, "Tenneblind."

"Tenneblind?" Eli asked.

"Yep, and when you get to the end of your journey and you take your blindfold off and you become a man, you can call yourself Tennessee." Hoary Jory laughed at the pun. He laughed much too hard.

The fire dwindled and they sat in silence for a while. Then Hoary Jory stood up. "Well, thanks for the company, Tenneblind," he said, "but I must get some sleep." He patted Eli on the shoulder.

Eli sat alone, staring into the coals, watching them strum with heat, with a multitude of reds and oranges and yellows. More shades than Eli thought possible. He picked up his grandfather's journal and read.

September 16th, 1933

We went to the church today, me and Grandad. Mother doesn't
go because she says you have to be born twice to be a member of
the church, and she says being born once in a lifetime should
be enough for anyone. The preacher talked about the cleansing
power of water. Mother says the water doesn't cleanse you,
not like the preacher said it does, at least. She says the water
strengthens you, connects you to other lands and spirits. I asked
Dad and he doesn't seem interested either way. He said water
is for drinking, and anyone who says otherwise doesn't know
anything. He laughed when he said it and winked at me and
told me never to tell Mother he said that.

I think maybe the preacher and Mother and Dad are all
right. Water does cleanse, and if you drink it, it strengthens
you. Who knows?

The revival was fun, though. Most of our neighbors were
there. The younger kids hopped and danced, and we all sang
and clapped. When the day was a little less hot, we all went
outside. Grandad sat under the shade of a tree with a bunch
of our neighbors. One of our neighbors played a banjo, and
Grandad sang a few songs. He has a deep voice. It doesn't
carry through the air, but instead walks along the ground, its
feet in the soil. That's how I imagined it, at least. Several of
the boys and girls square danced. I didn't, though. I sat in the
grass and looked out on the country. The sky seemed bigger
than possible, like a giant blue bowl dropped over us.

October 28th, 1933

Dad and I loaded up the pickup today and went to the store to sell some things, butter and eggs and such. We also took our neighbor's stuff in because they don't have a truck and it's a long trip in a wagon. We make it to the store in a couple of hours in our pickup, but for many of the farmers, Grandad included before we moved here with our pickup, going to the store means a day on the road. Dad is one of the only people here with a pickup. Lots of people had them in Knoxville. It's strange that more people here don't. I guess they don't have the money to buy them, though.

We traded a few chickens and eggs and butter for sugar and coffee and things, and I got a new pair of shoe laces. They got everything you need.

Dad picked up a paper at the store. In it, there was a photo of two women washing clothes in a tub outside. It made Dad angry. He says the people of Coal Creek are being misrepresented, says we look ignorant in the papers, but I'm not sure what he means. We do wash our clothes in a tub. I told him that, and he said it's not what you do that counts. It's how people perceive what you do that counts. I'll have to think on that some more. To me, it seems one is the same as the other. But Dad is a smart man, and I'm sure if he says a thing is true, it's true.

Eli closed the journal, wrapped it in the red silk handkerchief, and sealed it in the bag. He put the fire out and slipped into the shelter, careful not to wake Hoary Jory.

Eli woke up the next morning to the muffled sound of his watch beeping in his sleeping bag. He looked at the ceiling, where his pack hung from the rafters. He blinked the world into focus and sat up. He was alone in the shelter. Hoary Jory was gone.

The white blazes became hypnotic, and time became meaningless. Eli walked. He walked up and he walked down. He walked through fields and through forests. He walked through high woods, where the trees were barely getting their summer coats and the air cooled his lungs, and he walked through low woods, where the trees were in full bloom and pollen pasted his sweaty skin and skinny mosquitoes stalked him.

The only thing that mattered was moving forward. It became like a game of Pac-Man. He ate up the white blazes, and the third day passed with relative ease. His heels hurt, and his shoulders were tense under the weight of his pack, but he hiked around twenty miles with little incident. He stopped at Cherry Gap Shelter, a cinderblock structure with a tin roof. Its walls were covered in graffiti, mostly trail names and dates and inspirational quotes.

That night, with his headlamp on, Eli read from his grandfather's journal.

February 12th, 1934

A man from the Tennessee Valley Authority came to talk to
Grandad today. We all sat on the porch and listened to him.
The TVA is building a dam. The land agent said it will supply
electricity to hundreds of thousands of people and will also help
stop the floods and erosion that cause damage and death. The
land agent said the dam would flood Grandad's land, though.
He said all the people of Coal Creek, which he called Norris
Basin, had to move. The government is buying all the land here.
　　Grandad has lived in Coal Creek his whole life. His dad
and mother and their dad and mother are buried on this farm,
and so is one of his sisters and her infant son, who both died in
childbirth. This is his land. He doesn't want to leave, and he said
he won't. He thanked the man for coming and then went down to
the south field, to the bunkhouses. He rarely goes down there.
　　After Grandad left, Dad and the land agent talked alone.
Well, they thought they were alone. I was leaning against the
house around the corner. The land agent said the TVA needed
local help to get the dam built. They needed men of reason
to talk to the hard old men. Those were his words, the land
agent's. Hard old men.
　　After the man left, Dad and I sat on the porch. He said the
TVA is here to help us, and he thinks it's a good idea to sell the
land. He said that sometimes you have to think of the greater
good, you have to put your neighbors ahead of yourself, you
have to leave your home so that someone else can have one.

When Grandad came back, Dad told me to go help Mother.
I think he wanted to talk to Grandad alone.

February 21st, 1934

Dad went to the neighbor's today. He walked, which was
unusual. He normally drives down there as it's a bit of a trek.
When I asked him if I could go, he said no. He said he had
business with them and that I should stay and help Mother.

When Dad got back, he sat on the porch with Grandad.
They talked about the TVA for a long time. Dad supports
the TVA. He says it's a new era, and it's going to change
everything for us. Grandad said Dad went soft in Knoxville,
got used to having money in his pockets and forgot what's
important. Dad shook his head. He said it's not about money.
Grandad cut him off. He waved his hand toward the north
field, where corn and tobacco grow, and asked Dad why he
needed more than this. Dad didn't answer, and Grandad just
rocked in his chair and stared at the north field.

While Eli ate oatmeal the following morning, his mind
wandered to the land near his home. The woods there were
his. He wondered what he would do if someone asked him to
leave them, told his mom and him that they had to go. He didn't

76

think he would take it very well. He liked the land where he lived, but was it different than the land he was hiking across? The trees where he sat were just trees. The forest there was different than the land behind his home only because he knew that land, was familiar with it. The trees were the same type, their branches stretched toward the same sky.

Eli squinted at the sky. It didn't look happy. It was gray as far as he could see. It was probably gray above his home, too. He cleaned his breakfast pot and packed for the day.

By mid-afternoon the rain started pouring. Eli stopped beneath the limbs of a large tree and pulled on his rain jacket. He wiped the water from his face and hair. It was an Appalachian bath. After all, he hadn't showered in four days. He laughed at that. His mom was always telling him to shower more. Perhaps the birds and squirrels felt the same way and had asked the sky to clean him. It felt good. It washed the salt off his face and the dirt off his hands. But it made hiking difficult.

The rocks and fallen trees slicked with water, and the dirt turned to deep mud. Eli's boots sank into it. With each step, his feet lifted with a slurp and plopped down with a squish, and the mud splashed onto his legs. Several times, Eli almost fell, his boots sticking in the trail. He needed a walking stick.

He picked up fallen branches near the path, but they all were too thin, too short, or too fat. So he walked into the woods, stopping here and there to examine a branch and glancing periodically behind him to ensure he was walking in a fairly straight line off the trail. The last thing he wanted was to lose the white blazes again.

The water splattered on the leaves and flowed down the ferns in streams. It cleaned the mud from his legs. Not far off the trail, he picked up a long branch that fit his grip. He ripped a few of the smaller branches from it and then stood it up. It was about fifteen feet tall and fairly straight. If he could break it at the right spot, he would have a good walking stick. He gripped the limb in two hands and whacked it against a tree. Half the branch broke off and bounced to the ground.

He held the remaining piece next to him like a wizard staff. It was still much taller than him, though. He turned the staff over, debating which end to break off next. Having made his decision, he swung the limb like a bat. It connected with the tree and vibrated his hands and forearms, but it didn't break. He wiped the water from his face and prepared to swing the branch again when he saw something move to his right.

The Yunwi Tsunsdi, that was his first thought. He was wrong. Less than twenty yards away, three black bear cubs scurried up a tree like hairy little worms. Their mother stood between them and Eli, water dripping down her fur.

Eli froze. He forgot about the stick in his hand. He forgot about the rain. He forgot about the trail and his grandfather and father. All he saw was the bear, and all he felt was his heart thumping. Time leapt away from him. The rain slowed, splashing on the branches, rolling off the leaves, dripping down his face. The bear's matted fur shook. Her muscles flexed.

She lunged forward.

Eli ran. He didn't think. His body did everything for him. His legs rose and fell, automated pumps. His arms gripped the straps of his pack, which bounced on his back. He zipped through the trees. The ferns slapped his legs and his boots slammed into the muddy forest floor.

He didn't notice the ground drop from beneath him. All he knew was one moment he was running and the next he wasn't. The world became a jumble of green and brown, leaves and bark, ferns and mud.

Dee sat by the window, staring into the woods. The rain poured down. Somewhere out there, her baby was alone, probably wet and hungry. It had been four days since Eli left, and she'd read the note hundreds of times.

The phone rang and she jumped up to answer it. "Did you find him?" she blurted into it.

"It's Susan. I'm just calling to see if you've eaten anything since Eli ran off." Susan was their neighbor. She lived just a few miles down the road and was also married to Ben.

"Oh, hi Susan," Dee said. "Thanks for calling. I'm fine. I just—" Dee's voice trembled with tears and her back muscles shuddered as if she was cold.

"I'm comin' over," Susan said.

Dee set the phone on the table and rubbed her eyes with her shirt sleeve. Susan came in a few minutes later. She didn't knock. She just came in and put a kettle of water on the stove for tea.

Eli raised his head, half expecting the bear to follow him down the ravine. It didn't. In fact, the bear probably hadn't followed him at all. It probably had faked him out, and Eli should have known better. His father had told him what to do if he ever met a bear in the woods. He was supposed to slowly back away. Slip from the bear's territory as calmly as he'd entered it. Eli did everything wrong. He let his fear control him.

Because of that, he lay at the bottom of deep gulch with his face in the mud. He rolled over and pain flew up his left leg. He sucked in a quick breath and bit his lip. Nothing was broken or bent out of place, but blood poured from a gash about an inch long and a quarter inch deep. Rain watered down the blood and carried it away.

Eli shook himself from his pack and sat up. He reached into his bag and grabbed one of his spare t-shirts. He pressed the shirt into the cut and then pulled it away. Fresh blood flooded the wound, turning the whitish-pink flesh red. He tied the shirt around his leg. Once he was back on the trail, he'd either find a shelter or set up his tent to get out of the rain. After that, he could clean the wound and bandage it.

He stood. The world swayed. He looked up the hill he'd just fallen down. It was covered in ferns. He wasn't surprised he hadn't seen the ground slope. The whole forest floor was a blanket of plants.

He lifted his pack onto his shoulders and put some weight on his injured leg. It hurt, but he could walk. He followed the ravine for a ways. It was deep and steep and covered in wet green. After putting some distance between him and the bear, he started climbing. He slipped several times. The mud clung to his rain jacket and shorts. It smeared his hands, obscured the creases on his knuckles, knuckles similar to his grandfather's. His fingers were slimmer, younger, less hairy than his grandfather's hands, but they had the same twists and bulges. With enough work, enough grease and earth rubbed into their palms, and enough nicks on their knuckles, his hands would grow to be just like his grandfather's.

When he made it to the top of the hill, he walked back to the trail, cutting slightly south to give the bear plenty of space.

Back on the trail, he followed the white blazes for half a mile or so before seeing signs for a campsite. It was several hours before dark, but he needed to clean his leg. More than that, he wanted to take off his muddy clothes, eat something, and fall asleep. He just wanted to stop.

At the campsite, several massive maples stood in a row. Their twisted branches reached toward the sky. Eli followed the trees away from the campsite. No one else was there, but it was early in the day. He didn't want company that night.

He pitched his tent in a small, secluded clearing. As he pushed the poles together, the water splattered on his back and head. Lightning boomed and he jumped. It was incredibly loud, close.

He shook as much water and mud as he could from his pack, tossed it inside the tent, and climbed in after it. The rain drummed on the taught nylon, repetitive yet chaotic. It filled the small space with gushing sound.

He took off his clothes. The cuts from the car crash covered his right side. The few remaining scabs were wet from the rain. He wrung out his shirt and pants as best he could under the tent's small entrance cover. Water dripped off him and his gear and pooled in the corner. He took out the first aid kit and removed the shirt from his leg. It looked like someone had scooped a bit of his flesh out with a spoon.

He dug through the first aid kit for hydrogen peroxide. It contained none. There were, however, a few antiseptic wipes. Eli ripped one open. In the cut, the flesh was pink and exposed. He took a breath and pressed the wipe into the wound. His leg tightened with pain. It crept up his calf, over his thigh, and into his stomach, where it floated like a bubble. The antiseptic wipe turned from white to red. Eli opened another wipe and repeated the process. After he finished cleaning the cut, he pressed a gauze pad into it to stop the bleeding. Then he squeezed a glob of antibacterial cream onto the exposed flesh and taped a clean gauze pad over it. The pain slowed from a high-pitched scream to a strumming beat, and Eli lay down. His hunger was gone. He closed his eyes and listened to the water flow over the tent.

For a while, Eli walked along sleep's edge, somewhere between dream and reality. The sound of the rain buzzed around him, seeming to grow louder and throb in time with the pain in his leg. He stared into the darkness of his mind and then slipped into sleep.

"They'll find him, Dee," Susan said. "Heck, most likely, he'll return on his own in a day or two."

"It's already been four days," Dee said. The tears had dried on her cheeks. "I don't understand how he could do this, why he would do this."

Susan shook her head. "He's young. He's confused. He doesn't know how to deal with the loss of—" She bit her lip.

"Sam." Dee said it for her.

"I'm sorry."

Dee nodded and looked into her cup. Steam swirled off the surface of the tea and disappeared into the air.

"Ben said the forest rangers and police from here, North Carolina, and into Virginia have his photo now." Susan traced the wood grain on the table. "But I doubt he's even that far away. He's probably hiding just back there, in the woods somewhere." Susan nodded out the window. "That's what Ben thinks."

Dee looked into the woods. The leaves and trunks dripped with rain. "He's not back there. He's on the Appalachian Trail. I know he is. He's been talking about it for so long. His father filled his head with all these ideas."

"Just 'cause he wanted to hike it doesn't mean he can, Dee. If he's on the AT, he'll probably get tired in another day or two and call you."

Dee smiled, possibly for the first time in over a month. "You don't know my son."

The forest crept around Eli's tent. The ferns unfurled and fondled the nylon. They curled around the poles and lifted, carrying the tent and Eli into the trees. The branches reached out and pulled the threads from the seams, peeling the tent, exposing Eli like soft fruit. The tent fell to the forest floor, discarded and as useless as a banana skin.

Eli drifted through the forest on the branches, handed from one tree to the next, on and on. Each branch that curled around him was marked with a white blaze. The forest carried him like this for miles and days, all the way to Maine and up Mount Katahdin. At the top of the mountain, a giant tree grew, a tree that stretched above the atmosphere, its leaves blowing with the rotation of the Earth. Its branches reached out and received Eli. Its bark flowed with light. Eli drifted down its surface and onto the ground.

He stood before the tree. His father's and grandfather's names were inscribed in the bark. Eli felt the black-handled pocketknife in his palm. He stepped toward the tree and raised his hand to carve his own name. But before his blade touched the tree, rain poured from the sky and washed the names from the trunk. They spilled on to the ground and soaked into the dirt with the water.

Eli dropped the knife and fell to his knees. He started digging, searching for the names. He dug like an animal, scooping the soil with his hands. It packed under his nails and coated his arms. Then his fingers felt something soft, something fleshy. He scraped the earth away until he realized what it was. He pulled his hands back and stood up. He was in the cemetery where his father was buried. He was standing in his father's grave.

Eli woke up crying. The sun had set and darkness filled the tent. He lay on his side. He felt the tears drip from his face. The rain beat at the nylon bubble surrounding him. He could almost feel the empty space between him and the rain, a space filled with loss.

Then something scraped on the tent. Eli's sobbing stopped but the tears continued gliding down his cheeks. Something clawed at the entrance. He held his breath. It was too dark to see anything. He reached out, feeling for his pack. His fingers felt the strap and followed it up to the opening. He dug into his gear, his eyes spilling tears. His fingers felt the cool handle of the flashlight. He pulled it out and clicked the button. The walls of the tent glowed. Eli held the light and listened.

The scraping picked up speed. He covered the light with his fingers, illuminating his veins and tendons. His heart seemed about to rattle his ribs loose. His only defense was his wrist rocket, and he didn't have any rocks for it.

Then he remembered the pocketknife. He pulled it out and opened its blade. He gripped it, his fingers shaking against its surface.

There could be anything out there: a bear or a pack of wolves, circling and hungry, smelling him through the tent, ready to rip him open. Or it could be some crazy person, insane and ready to kill him. Or it could be something worse. Eli was afraid to think it, but he couldn't stop, he couldn't stop his imagination from filling the tent, filling the forest with monsters. It could be U`tlun'ta, the Spear-Finger. His throat burned with the image of her: her bony rock-like skin, her long forefinger reaching out, scratching at the tent. She'd come for him. She would draw him in, and then she would stab him with her finger and eat his liver.

He saw her finger press against the nylon and trace a line down its surface. He held his breath, listening to the scraping, waiting for the zipper to peel open. He waited for U`tlun'ta to smile through the flap and creep into the tent with him, cooing and smelling of rot. He held his breath until his lungs were about to burst, until his fear was uncontainable, and then he screamed, "Go away!"

But the scraping continued. Eli curled into the corner of his tent. He held the flashlight in one hand and the pocketknife in the other, and he waited to die. Seconds slammed by, their passage almost audible. The rain fell, filling the space with white noise. He felt trapped, alone, terrified. He cried. Tears of fear, tears of anger, tears of mourning. His dad was never coming back, and he'd fled, left his mom. He felt terrible. He felt like dying. He needed help.

He scrambled to his pack, dropping the light and the knife. He pulled his phone, which he'd put into a sandwich bag for dry keeping, out and turned it on. He would call his mom. He would call her and tell her where he was and she would come to him, and the pain and the fear would float away. The screen lit up, and Eli waited for the phone to get reception. But no bars appeared. He dialed his mom's number anyway and pressed call. The number blinked on the screen and the call ended before it started. Eli pressed call again, and the same thing happened.

He would have no help, not that night. He closed his eyes, clutched the flashlight and the pocketknife, and waited. Spirits and witches and monsters swam through the dark of his mind. He tried to push them out, but the more he ignored them the more they fought. He laid his head on his pack and waited for it all to stop. Eventually, sleep crept back into the tent, and the monsters fled back into the forest.

When Eli woke up, the tent was filled with morning light. He clicked the flashlight off and closed the pocketknife. He unzipped the tent flap an inch at a time, half expecting U`tlun'ta to be standing outside. He saw nothing but the forest. The rain had stopped and the sky had cleared during the night. He crawled outside. Hanging from a tree, a broken branch dangled. Small limbs poked from it and pressed on the tent.

Eli felt foolish. That was what he'd been so terrified of—a branch. He felt foolish for trying to call his mom, for being so afraid of nothing.

A titmouse landed on the tent. It seemed to look right at him as if it was asking him what he was going to do next. It called a few times and fluttered away. Eli heard Hoary Jory's voice: "Don't take the blindfold off until morning. Keep your pace steady and your mind free of fear."

He had failed to do that. His father would be disappointed in him, but he had weeks ahead of him to make up for it, weeks ahead of him to make his father proud. Next time he was tested, he wouldn't let fear control him.

That morning, the trail clung to his boots. Eli felt like he was walking on a pond, and if he slowed for an instant, he would begin to sink and the water would swallow him. Only, the pond was the muddy earth. Walking was difficult, made him flex his muscles more. In time with his steps, the divot in his calf filled with pain that spilled into his leg. Fill and spill, fill and spill; that was how the hiking went that morning.

Half an hour after he started, he passed a shelter. If he'd walked just one more mile the previous day, he wouldn't have had to stay in his tent. He breathed deeply as he passed the trail to the shelter. Above him, a few thin clouds stretched through the blue, tinting it white.

As he climbed in elevation, the forest thinned, turning to grass. He could see for miles and miles in all directions. The trail was clean and coated in gray gravel. It looped through the fields, which were short and green in some areas and tall and yellow in others. To the north, a large bald peak stood. It sloped toward the horizon in both directions until it was consumed by hills and ridges. Directly above him, the sky was deep blue. Around the peak, though, it lightened and turned purple and then white, a haze like a halo.

Eli walked toward it. He let his hand glide along the tops of the stalks of yellow grass. They tickled his palms, rubbed and brushed the pads on his fingers as they played in the wind. The field swayed together, the grass danced, and for a moment Eli's mind danced with it. As he reached the peak's summit, he let the music of the landscape fill his ears.

Eli sat down. He sat in nature's concert hall. The bows warmed on the strings. The brass pressed the players' lips. The reeds split the air. The birds and insects sang their songs, buzzing and tweeting and chirping. Their voices carried through the field, through the dirt, and through the sky. The grass played percussion in the wind, swaying and shaking and rubbing. It was a slow orchestra practiced and performed outside of time. They had no audience, nor did they care about one. They played for themselves. They played because that's all they knew to do. They played because stopping meant death.

The world vibrated with sound and with life, and Eli forgot where he was. He forgot who he was and how he'd arrived there. He forgot everything outside of what was happening in front of him. For that moment he lived like a bird lives, like a bee lives, like a blade of grass lives: completely absorbed in the present, unaware of what things were called and how they functioned.

He looked out across the flowing field. Something moved in it. Something short and quick, it split the grass. Running or crawling, Eli wasn't sure. He couldn't see it. He could only see where it displaced the grass. It zigged and zagged toward the horizon, over the slope of the mountain, and out of sight.

Then the buzzing died down, and the world regained its labels. The grass, for a moment nothing more than long bits of earth blowing in the wind, became grass again, and the birds, momentarily just bits of life fluttering in the sky, became birds again.

Eli surveyed the land. There were no cities, no towns, nothing but mountains as far as he could see. From where he sat, the world appeared unpopulated by people. It was just Eli. Eli and a few birds, and perhaps the Yunwi Tsunsdi.

He stood. The world tilted. The clouds and earth jumped, overlapping each other. For an instant Eli was uncertain what was up and what was down. Then everything fell back into place, and he sat again. His vision blurred. His thoughts felt disconnected from his brain. His calf hurt, but at the same time he felt no pain. He seemed to float, detached, somewhere behind his head. He drank some water and breathed. He heard the air move in and out, but he felt no breath. After a little while, he stood and started walking again. But it was different. He felt different, like he wasn't actually walking, like someone had thrown on the autopilot. His body became a machine, his movement mechanical.

As he descended the mountain, he felt his thoughts also descend from some high, unknown place. The feeling of disconnection left him. It was replaced by hunger, which flowed into him from the ground up, twitching in his legs, tingling in his fingers. He stopped and ate lunch, taking note that his food supply was getting low.

After eating, he crossed several small wooden bridges, some not much more than a plank laid over a creek, and his leg began to throb. He stopped at the bank of one of the wider creeks and pulled the bandage off. The cut was red, its edges swollen. He poured water from his canteen over the wound. It picked up the dry blood and streamed down his leg in pink lines. He put another glob of antibacterial cream into it and covered it with a fresh bandage.

He walked the rest of the afternoon, hoping he would find a side trail or road leading to a town where he could refill his food supply. None came, though.

As night crept in, Eli saw an old wooden shelter. It had three steps leading into a wide doorless entrance, and its right side stood on blocks. A fire pit was dug into the ground near it. Eli checked his watch. He could either stay there for the night or hike off the trail and pitch his tent. The black interior of the building didn't look very inviting.

"Anybody in there?" Eli called. No reply came, so he crept up the steps and poked his head in. It was dry inside. It would do. He pulled his pack off and set about making a fire.

March 1st, 1934

The land agent returned today and Grandad asked only two
questions. This dam, he said, it'll help a whole lot of people?
The representative said, yes sir, a whole lot of folks. Grandad
waved his hand at his farm and said, but the people who live
here, we got to pay the price by moving? I could tell Grandad
knew what answer was coming.

The man said the TVA would compensate us for the land
and help us relocate if necessary, but he said that, yes, they're
asking families here to make a sacrifice for the rest of the
country. Grandad nodded his head and said all right. He told
the land agent to tell us what we got to do to help. He looked
different than usual, though. There was something in his face
I've never seen before. Sadness, I suppose.

Then Grandad signed some papers, and the difference I saw
on his face flowed into the rest of his body. Grandad is a tall
man, thin and broad shouldered. But as he signed those papers,
pressed them against the side of the house, the house he was
born in, the house his father was born in, the house where he
raised his family and watched them live and die, he seemed to
wither, wither like a stalk of grass that can no longer take the
summer heat.

After the land agent left, Grandad walked into the north
field. Dad started to follow him, but Grandad waved him
away. Dad came back up on the porch and told me to go inside,
but I lingered, I watched. Grandad took off his hat and sat

down in the field. He cupped a handful of soil and let it fall from his hand.

April 5th, 1934

There'll be a funeral soon. One of our neighbors hung himself today. The mood is odd, like there's something thick in the air, and everyone feels it, but no one will talk about it. Grandad called in all the men, all the field hands and tenants. The men took their hats off when he told them. Then he told them to take the rest of the day and spend it with their wives and children, and if they didn't have any, they should come up to the Big House and have supper with us.

I never saw so many somber eyes. Most of the men shuffled their feet in the dust and walked away, but a few stayed, talking to each other in low voices. After a while, Grandad waved them up onto the porch and told them to get out of the sun. We all sat together. Usually, when you get a few of the tenant farmers up at the Big House, there's a lot of talk and laughter, fiddle playing, and checker games. Today there was none. Grandad just stared into the north field. His rocking chair was still. The men sat on the steps. Dad leaned against the door jam. No one even looked at each other.

July 7th, 1934

The TVA men came today and started digging up our family's graves. It feels strange. Grandad just watched them, just sat on the porch and watched them work. I've never seen him sit idly by and watch while someone else broke a sweat. But today he did.

Mother and I went for a walk through the north field while the TVA men dug. She didn't want to be around it, said they should let the people rest where they were. Water or no water, the people should stay where they were buried. It does seem strange to move the bodies so that they won't be under water once the dam is finished.

Mother was quiet for a long time then. We just walked, side by side, along the rows of tobacco. She pulled a leaf off a plant and rubbed it in her fingers. She wiped a few tears away. She tried to hide them from me, but I saw. Then she said she was sorry, for everything. She waved her hand at the north field and said she was sorry the earth was so ragged, so awful. She apologized to me, apologized for the world I was born into. It seems like a strange thing to apologize for, as if she had any control over the earth.

I told her everything would be all right, everything would be fine. The Yunwi Tsunsdi would watch over us as we moved. She laughed and smiled at that.

The following morning, the AT spilled onto a highway. Eli needed to restock his food. He saw no signs for towns in either direction, so he picked one at random and started walking. Within a minute a truck slowed next to him. Eli ignored it, hoping the driver would just go past, hoping it wasn't a forest ranger or off-duty cop. This was stupid, he thought. He should have just kept on the trail. He knew the Forest Service and police were looking for him. But he really had no choice. He needed food.

The driver stopped the truck and leaned over to the passenger door and opened it. "You headin' into town?" he asked. He had a red beard and wore a flannel shirt.

Eli almost laughed. The guy looked like a cliché lumberjack. Instead of laughing, he just nodded his head.

"Well, get in."

The interior of the cab smelled like dust and mold.

"You hikin' the AT?" the man asked.

"Yes," Eli said, then added, "With my dad. I'm just going into town for food while he waits for me." Eli glanced at the man, who kept his eyes on the road.

"I can drop you at the country store up here," he said.

He must have bought the story. "That'd be great."

"I hiked the AT some. Roan Mountain's a pretty good climb. You cross it yet?"

"Not sure," Eli said.

The man glanced at him. His eyebrows turned down. "Not sure? Don't you got a map?"

"My dad carries it. I'm just not sure which one was Roan Mountain." Eli tried to save the conversation from turning on him.

97

"It's the one that left you breathless." The man laughed. He sounded like a woodchuck dying. "It's just south of here. The air's pretty thin up there."

The truck stopped by a sign that marked Highway 19. The man pointed past it to a building that could have been a store but could also have been a house. "They've got trail food in there," the man said.

Eli thanked him and slid out. The tires spun up a cloud of dust as the truck pulled away. Eli turned to the building. There were some flyers and advertisements and things hanging on one window. Eli took the sandwich bag that contained his money out of his pack.

Inside, a few dusty rows of canned and dried goods stood next to a wall of coolers. Eli grabbed more pasta and oatmeal, dried fruit, trail mix, and granola bars. He also grabbed a fistful of candy bars and a big bag of beef jerky. He hadn't eaten any meat since he left his house. It sounded incredibly good. Finally, he snagged a pint of ice cream. He felt hungry prior to entering the store, but suddenly he felt voracious. He wanted to rip the ice cream open and eat it with his hands.

He set the basket full of his food on the counter. A man came out of the rear of the shop and mumbled a greeting without looking at him. His double chin draped over his neck, and his eyes were just a fraction too far apart. He looked like a bullfrog about to croak. He breathed heavily through his mouth as he turned each item over, looking for price tags and punching buttons on a cash register that belonged in an '80s movie. A sign next to the register read, "Cash Only." Beside this, there was a small rack of maps. Eli took one labeled "The Appalachian Trail: Tennessee and North Carolina" and another labeled "The Appalachian Trail: Virginia." The man bagged Eli's goods, finally looking up at him as he asked for thirty-six dollars and eighty-eight cents.

Eli pulled two twenties from the sandwich bag and held them out to the man, whose eyebrows slowly rose as recognition spread across his face.

"Hey, you're that Tennessee boy, aren't you?" the man asked, his chin wobbling. "The county sheriff came through here just this mornin' askin' if I'd seen you."

Eli wasn't sure what to do. He was still holding the money out, but the man wasn't taking it. He tried to lie. "Not sure what you're talking about. I'm hiking with my dad. Just need to get these groceries and go. He's waiting for me." His hand wavered a little bit, the money in his fingers. He wasn't prepared for this.

"No," the man said. "I recognize your face. The sheriff left a picture of you." He reached under the counter and withdrew a flyer with Eli's face on it. "You're him." The man pointed to the flyer. "Stay there," he said, turning for the phone.

Eli dropped the money, grabbed the bag of groceries, and ran. His pack bounced on his shoulders. His wounded calf pumped pain into his leg. He ran down the highway about fifty yards and then cut up into the woods and kept going until his lungs filled with needles.

He stopped to catch his breath as sweat burst from his skin. He sat on a stump. Through the trees he could see pastures speckled with cattle and farm equipment. His legs felt a little wobbly from sprinting, but he couldn't rest for long. He needed to put some more distance between him and the store. He unfolded the Tennessee and North Carolina map. He found Highway 19 where it intersected the AT, where he'd left the trail. He traced his finger along the highway to where he believed the store was, then north into the woods. He probably hadn't run more than five hundred yards. If he walked northwest about a mile and a half, he would be back on the trail. But the trail followed several roads there, and if the sheriff was looking for him, then he needed to stay off the roads. He looked up. In the distance, cattle grazed. He could stay off the roads if he cut through farmland.

He slipped through several pastures, stopping after passing roads to find himself on the map and make sure he wasn't going the wrong direction. The temperature in the open was hotter than in the woods. He drank the last bits of water he had in one canteen and shook the other. It was only about half full. He would need to refill them before the day was done. Sweat dripped down his back. He took a sip from the second canteen, and his stomach groaned. He couldn't take it any longer. His hunger buzzed in his legs and shoulders. He glanced around. There was a small house a few hundred yards away and a cluster of trees near him. He walked toward the trees.

He sat in the shade and ripped the lid off the ice cream. It was a sloppy melting mess, but he ate it anyway, the entire container, slurping the milk and sugar from the bottom. He'd been on the trail for six days, hiking between twelve and twenty miles each day. That was a lot of burned calories, and Eli was thin to begin with. He felt the sugar almost instantly. It flooded his muscles. He drank another gulp of water. His canteen was light, and it would be several hours before he set up camp for the night. Unless he wanted to stop for an hour and boil water, he needed to refill before getting back on the trail.

He walked toward the house. He had no intention of knocking on the door, but he bet there was a faucet on the outside of it somewhere. He would just fill his canteens and go. The people probably were out working anyway. After all, it was mid-day.

The house was surrounded by a short fence. A pickup was parked under an apple tree, but no apples were on the tree yet. Eli checked to make sure no one was around, and he hopped the fence. He kept his distance from the house, scanning for a spigot. Rounding the corner, he saw a hose coiled near the back porch.

The water gushed out, clean and clear. Eli drank some of it directly and then filled one canteen. He twisted the lid off the other and began filling it just as the screen door on the porch creaked open and a bald man stepped out of the house.

"Can I help you?" he asked.

Eli panicked. He dropped the hose, dropped the canteen, and turned for his pack. He scrambled to get it on as the man laughed behind him.

"I didn't mean to startle you, boy." He kept laughing.

Eli started walking away from the house.

"Hey, wait," the man called.

This was it, he thought. He was done. Sure, he could run. But the woods were a long way away. He wouldn't reach them before the man caught him, drove up next to him in the pickup in front of the house. His journey would end there. His father and grandfather would be disappointed in him.

"You forgot your water," the man said.

Eli turned. His canteen lay in the grass.

"I really didn't mean to give you a scare," the man said. "I was just sitting down to lunch and saw you out here. You hiking the Appalachian?"

"Yes, sir," Eli said. The man apparently hadn't heard about the runaway Tennessee boy.

"We get a lot of hikers passing through town. Not too many this far off the trail, though. You must've been thirsty."

Eli nodded. "Yes, sir, I was."

The man waved him over. "Replenish your water. I don't mind."

Eli wiped the sweat from his forehead. He squatted in the yard and filled his canteen. "Sorry to come on your property, but I was really low on water."

The man looked down at Eli from the porch. He was older than Eli had first guessed. "By the looks of it, you're really hungry too," he said. "You look like you haven't eaten anything in months. I suppose hikin' will do that to you, though. Why don't you come in for a meal? I got plenty."

"I couldn't do that, sir."

"Sure you can," the old man said. "I got beef stew and cheese and crackers. Come on in."

Eli's body fluttered with hunger. He took his pack off and followed the man into the house.

The screen door snapped closed behind Eli. He smelled the stew. His stomach responded in a low tone. A few pairs of shoes littered the entrance of the home. Eli took off his boots. They were caked in mud. His socks left wet prints on the wood floor, and Eli was sure he stank, but the man waved him in anyway.

In the kitchen, there was a small table next to a window. The man pulled a chair out for Eli. From where Eli sat, he could see the living room walls were lined with black and white photos: young, dusty men smiling and holding shovels; a girl posing by a tractor, her dress and hair caught in the wind; a dozen or more thin children and teens standing on a porch, staring at the camera.

"It looks like you were in quite a scuffle," the old man said, sitting down.

Eli wasn't sure what he was talking about.

"The scrapes on your face. Did it happen on the trail?"

Eli felt the road rash on his forehead, temple, and cheek.

The scabs were almost all gone, but the scars remained. "I was in a car accident," Eli said, "before I started hiking."

"Dangerous business, driving. I hope everyone was all right."

Eli said nothing.

The man filled a bowl to the brim with stew and set it in front of Eli, and he opened a package of crackers and slid them toward him as well. "Dig in," he said, pointing to the bowl.

Eli did just that. The stew was thick with tomatoes and beef. It was the best thing he'd ever tasted. He scooped it onto the crackers and munched them down, their salty surfaces wet with broth. With a mouthful of beef, Eli nodded to the photos in the living room and said, "That's a lot of pictures you got."

The old man turned and admired them. Liver spots covered his hands and head. A few thin bits of white hair were combed neatly over his scalp. Eli felt sorry for him, but wasn't quite sure why.

"It sure is," the man said, turning back to the table. "My wife loved to take photos. She had dozens of cameras in her life. It was her passion. And a very expensive hobby, I might add." The man smiled and chuckled. "There was a time when people didn't have hobbies. They had no time for them. What are your hobbies, son? Besides hiking through the wild."

Eli licked his lips. "Hiking, fishing, reading sometimes."

"Oh, well, that is quite a hobby," the old man said. "What do you read—you know, I never introduced myself." The man held out his hand. "Sorry to be so rude. Sometimes I think my mind's slipping. My name's Dalton."

Eli's spoon slipped into the bowl and he shook Dalton's hand. "Eli," he said. The man didn't know who he was, no use lying.

"Nice to meet you, Eli. So, as I was saying, what do you read?"

"Well, I've been reading my grandad's journal lately."

"Really? That is something. What did your grandaddy do?"

"He did lots. Before he retired and moved in with us, he worked for the TVA."

"You don't say? I worked for the TVA for many years before buying this place." Dalton waved a wrinkled hand to the land outside the window. "I fixed the power lines. What did he do?"

Eli blew on a spoonful of stew. "He worked on the dams, I think." Eli was only vaguely aware of what work his grandfather did. Since he could remember, his grandfather had mostly sat on the porch and drank tea and told stories about the Cherokee. Eli ate the bite of stew. It melted in his mouth and comforted his stomach.

"Well, working on the dams was admirable," the man said. "The TVA people, the engineers and the laborers, they did an important job. They worked to bring the people of the Tennessee Valley into the modern age. They worked to get power to people. There were a lot of poor people in the Tennessee Valley then. Still are, I suppose, God bless their souls. Back then, though, the land was at its limit. The men over-farmed it." The old man looked out the window.

Eli slurped some broth and ate a cracker.

"Wasn't their fault, though," Dalton said, looking back at Eli. "They were just trying to provide for their families. They were just doing what they'd always done. But you can only push the earth so far before she falls. Same goes for a man, though. They worked from sunrise to dark every day for nothing more than a few stalks of corn. Hell, when the depression hit, most of the farmers in the Tennessee Valley didn't know. Nothing changed for them."

His attention still half on the stew, Eli thought of his grandfather. The times must have been tough on him. Like his father said, Eli was lucky to have been born after all that.

"Disease swept the land," Dalton continued, "small pox, typhoid, malaria. It was awful for my parents. I lost three siblings." He held up three fingers and stared at them as if they were people seeds, as if he could plant his fingers in the ground and grow his family back. "Two brothers and a sister." Dalton's eyes focused beyond his fingers and out the window, into some distant land. "We needed help. Lots of it." He turned back to Eli. "But don't get me wrong, men were suspicious about what the TVA was here to do. Especially when they came asking for their homes."

Eli swallowed more stew. His stomach thanked him. "My grandfather lived in Coal Creek before the dam there was built. They had to move, but he said his grandfather gave up his land because it would help a lot of people."

The man laughed at Eli. "Son, it hasn't been called Coal Creek in more than 70 years. In any case, I suppose quite a few of the families did go willingly. Some of them didn't want to listen to outsiders, though. It was a matter of pride. The same thing happened when the TVA sent men to teach the locals new farming methods, farming methods that would help restore and maintain the land. Imagine you've been working your family's land your whole life, the land your daddy worked and your grandaddy worked. Then, one day, some hotshot comes in and starts telling you you're doing everything wrong." Dalton laughed. "You'd be likely to sock him one."

Dalton took a bite of stew. "So you know what the TVA did? They hired locals to champion the ideas. The farmers wouldn't listen to some guy from hundreds of miles away tell them how to farm the land they owned, so the TVA hired local men, respected men of the community, to bring the ideas in. Land is conquered—changed perhaps is a better word—from the outside in. Cultures, however, are changed from the inside out."

Eli ate another cracker dipped in the stew; its salty deliciousness stuck to the roof of his mouth.

"And this culture we had down here?" Dalton continued.

"Eli, I tell you, we were living in the Dark Ages. Prior to the Norris Dam, the floods raged almost every year and the people just dealt with it. They were hard people, with little to their name except the dirt on which they stood. And that was swept away by erosion. Hell, whole towns were swept away. The land was worthless here. Just seventy years ago, I tell you, it was worthless. Now look out there." Dalton pointed out the window. "Look at my pastures. Beautiful aren't they? In the 1930s that was all dust."

Eli slurped some broth from his spoon and looked out the window. The fields were indeed green and beautiful.

"But when the power came, it changed our lives." Dalton laughed, his eyes still looking out the window. "My daddy called it 'juice.' I remember when we first moved into a house with it. I flipped the lights on and off just as quickly as my fingers would let me." His eyes refocused. "I was used to candlelight, you see. But the juice, well, it flowed right from the wall. Flowed as easily as it did from oranges." His shoulders bounced as he chuckled. "At least I thought so at the time. I started working for the TVA in 1952. They trained me as a lineman, and I kept the juice flowing for forty years. I learned right quick that it was no easy task keeping all that power flowing."

Eli emptied his bowl and ate a cracker. He felt fuller than he ever had.

Dalton ladled some more stew into Eli's bowl. "It was all due to President Roosevelt," he continued. "My father loved him, but not everybody did, especially after the first TVA project, the Norris Dam. That dam submerged thousands and thousands of acres of land. People's lives were stolen from them. Like you said, many moved willingly, but I think anger grew in others as they were spread across the rest of the Tennessee Valley. The dam helped millions of people, but it stole the homes of thousands. That's how it works, though. Lots of bad has been done for the greater good." Dalton shook his head and smiled sadly. "And sometimes not for the good either. Hell, the Trail of Tears, for instance. Those people were told to walk. Just walk." He locked eyes with Eli. "And for what? Nothing. It's sad what man is capable of doing to himself." His gaze drifted back out the window. "At least the families living behind the Norris Dam moved for a reason. They packed their things into trunks and trucks and wagons, and they just set out. Some had places to go, others didn't, though."

Eli licked his lips as he finished his second bowl of stew, and glanced at the door. Silence spilled over the table. Just as Eli was about to say something, to thank the man and go, he spoke again.

"The dam was completed in 1936 and the land was flooded for good. It was the beginning of the future. The TVA hired lots of local people. They hired me. Who knows where I'd be without them. Submerged, perhaps, not under the water of Norris Dam, but under the dusty land. The TVA threw me a life vest when I was twenty-one years old, and I held onto it for forty years."

Eli ate another cracker. He really needed to get back on the trail, but he didn't know how to leave without being rude.

"And I hope I did good," Dalton said to no one. "People argue about how effective the TVA actually was. To that I ask, what was the alternative? We brought flood controls, electricity, fertilizers, running water, thousands of new jobs, new planting techniques. It's a hard call to make, but I think there really was only one choice. You've got to put the good of the majority first. In either case, what's done is done. You can only move forward and hope you don't have to repeat the mistakes of the past. Terrible deeds have happened in the name of progress, but are our lives better off because of it?" The man pointed out the window. "Just look out there. Today the Tennessee Valley is all green pastures and fat cattle, big cities and new developments. I'd say they made the right choice," he finished.

After a few seconds of silence, Eli jumped in. "Thank you for the stew, but I need to get back on the AT."

"Sure you don't want another bowl?" Dalton pointed at Eli's empty dish.

"I think if I did my belly would burst," Eli said.

Dalton laughed. "Good."

"Can you point me in the direction of the trailhead?" Eli stood.

"I can do you one better. How about I just drop you off there?"

Eli almost argued against it—but the sheriff. The sheriff might be driving up and down the roads. "As long as it's no trouble," he said.

Dee heard a car pull into the drive. She stepped onto the porch.

Ben climbed out of his cruiser. "Morning, Dee," he said.

She smiled thinly. She was afraid Ben had bad news, afraid the next words he said might be apologies and consolations.

"The North Carolina highway patrol received a call this morning. Your boy was spotted buying some groceries off the trail."

Dee melted. Eli was okay. "Are they bringing him back? Where is he?"

"Well, he ran," Ben continued. "But the forest rangers are looking for him in the surrounding woods, and they've notified the rangers to the north to set up a checkpoint on the trail. As long as he stays on it, they should have him back here by tomorrow or the next day." Ben shook his head. "I can't believe he made it that far, Dee."

Dee nodded. When Eli was determined to do something, nothing would stop him.

Eli woke up early and packed his tent. It was his seventh day on the trail. He ate oatmeal for breakfast again, while wishing he had more of Dalton's stew. He set out for another day of hiking, one more day closer to his goal.

Around mid-morning, Eli's right boot tore open. He walked off the trail a bit and sat in the woods. A bird called above him as he examined the damage. The inside seam had just split open. It was overworked, he supposed. He patched it with duct tape to keep out water. As he tore off strips of the tape, he heard voices on the trail.

"Well that was weird," a man said.

"Yeah, very," a woman said. "How long did they say he'd been missing?"

"A week."

Eli ducked behind the log he had been sitting on. They were talking about him.

"I hope they find him," the woman said.

"They will. They're stopping everyone." The man laughed. "For a minute I thought that ranger was going to pull me off the trail."

The woman also laughed. "You could pass as fourteen."

Their voices faded to the south. Eli stayed where he was, lying in the dirt. He wasn't sure what to do. From the sound of it, the forest rangers were not far up the trail, stopping everyone who passed. If he continued on his way, they would stop him and take him home. He felt the knife in his pocket. He needed to finish his hike. He needed to carve his name below his father's. Then there would be three generations of Suttons who had proved themselves on the Appalachian Trail. If he stopped there, he would disappoint his father.

He sat up and opened the map of Tennessee and North Carolina. He had passed Moreland Gap Shelter not long before. He found it on the map marked by a small black icon that resembled a shelter. From there, the AT curved west and then north toward Watauga Lake. Eli studied the map. The lake was big. It spread from the Watauga Dam, which had "TVA" written next to it, east almost all the way to the North Carolina border. If he left the trail and walked directly north, there was no way he could miss the lake. It was probably fifteen or twenty miles away. He could bypass the rangers and then get back on the trail at Watauga Lake. It would be easy. Heck, it might even save him time.

Eli took out his compass. The AT continued west-northwest from there. He turned north and slipped his compass into the cargo pocket of his shorts. He would need to check his direction often. Then he gathered a dozen small round stones and put those in his other pocket. He took his wrist rocket out and pulled it on. He loaded a stone and stretched the sling back. He sighted it on a tree, held his breath, and loosed it. The stone zipped through the air and smacked the tree. Eli supposed that if he ran into another bear, as a last resort, he could use the wrist rocket. It occurred to him that might be like spitting on a fire, but still, the sling made him feel safer.

The Cherokee National Forest was beautiful, beautiful and thick. Eli waded through a lake of ferns up to his waist. He climbed over fallen trees covered in inches of moss and passed boulders that wore coats of lichens. Vines lashed themselves to the trunks of trees and moss dripped from the branches. If he didn't keep moving, he had a feeling the forest would grow right over him, bury him, turn him into nothing more than a lump of lichens.

Everything around him was green. He could only see about ten yards in any direction, and the undergrowth slowed him down. Brush pressed against his legs and snagged his shorts. He tried to be like water and take the path of least resistance. With no landmark to walk toward and the sun blocked by a thick ceiling of leaves, it was easy to drift the wrong way. He checked his compass every few minutes and corrected his direction.

After a ways, he descended into a gully. He followed it for a bit, occasionally picking up a stone and firing it at a tree or rock, or just letting it go into the canopy, watching it punch through the leaves, and imagining it flying into the sky. Then the gully's walls grew shorter and shorter, eventually no taller than him, and the sound of water carried through the trees. A few minutes later, the gully dead ended at a river. It was fairly wide and fast moving. Eli stopped at the bank. The sounds of birds mixed with the gurgling water, sounding like a musical duet.

He ate a candy bar and stood by the river. He wasn't sure what the best way to cross was. To the west, the water fell over several large rocks and pooled at their base. The river was narrower there and it moved slower, but that meant it was deeper, too. In front of him, the river flowed faster, which meant it was shallower, but it was also wider. He picked up a rock the size of a bowling ball and tossed it. It splashed into the water. Eli guessed it was probably only two feet deep. He stuck the candy wrapper in his pack and his wrist rocket in his shorts.

The water flowed around his ankles and soaked his feet. It felt good after hiking and sweating all morning. About five feet from the bank, the river rose up to his knees and soaked his shorts. It swirled around him, trying to push him over. Eli tested each step, feeling for a steady place to put his weight. The river climbed past his knees, rushing around his thighs. He tightened the straps on his pack and took another few steps. The water dampened the bottom of his shirt and surrounded his waist, pushing and pushing. Eli's boots sunk into the soil. He jerked his feet from the earth and leaned forward to keep his balance. As he reached the middle of the river, the sound of flowing water surrounded him completely, and the singing of the birds faded away.

He took two more cumbersome steps, and then something brushed his leg. He pulled away from the touch and squinted into the water. He could see nothing but the white swirl of the river. Then he felt it again: something gliding around his leg, lingering. It didn't feel like a fish brushing past. Whatever it was, it coiled around his calf, like fingers. Eli pulled his feet from the soil, trying to get away from whatever was down there, but he slipped. The water pushed him over.

He thrashed his arms and tried to stand, fighting the weight of his pack, but the river rolled him over like a barrel. Water clouded his vision. He tried to turn over, but his pack pressed him down. He felt like a bug being held by the finger of a cruel child. The river filled his ears, nose, and mouth. It tasted coppery, smelled like mud, and the water's white noise dulled to a grumble that originated nowhere, a grumble that filled him, became internal—a thought more than a sound. He stared into the river. Bits of muck flowed past. A leaf and some sand slipped by against a backdrop of chocolate-brown soil.

Then the soil dropped away, deepening until Eli floated above a pit. The water ceased to flow. His thrashing stopped.

And out of the darkness faces formed, a dozen of them, one by one, outlined in white, with empty eyes and cavernous mouths. From behind the faces, hands reached up, grasping him. They gripped his wrists, shoulders, hair, jaw, and they pulled. They pulled him into the darkness of the river, into the hollow beneath the water.

He swirled with them, all groping hands and gaping eyes. And then the finger that had been pressing him down suddenly let go, and it was as if a hand reached into the water and wrapped around him. It scooped him from the black below the river.

He gasped for air and slapped the water. He spotted a large rock. The river split around it as he struggled to keep himself in line with it. The current was strong, but he grabbed on. His fingers slipped into a worn crevice. He slammed his feet into the riverbed and scrambled onto the rock, hugging it and spitting out water. He lay there a moment, coughing and sputtering and terrified.

There was a story his grandfather told him once about a haunted whirlpool. At the bottom of it, dozens of people lived. They would pull canoeists into the water. This was that river, he thought. That story was true. Eli shuddered.

When his breath was back, he plodded, dripping and shaking, to the other side of the river and fell onto the bank. A few clouds drifted through the blue. A bird landed on a branch above him and tweeted, unaware he had just almost died. He shook his head and started to laugh. That couldn't have just happened. His imagination was toying with him.

Then a curious sound floated from the white of the river, like laughter in the current. Eli snapped his head up and scanned the trees. It stopped almost as quickly as it started. He saw nothing, but he was sure he'd heard something. Perhaps it was the Yunwi Tsunsdi, watching him. He shook the water from his ears.

He pulled his arms from his pack and opened it. Water poured out. He turned it over and dumped his gear onto the dirt. His grandfather's journal wasn't wet; the plastic bag had kept the water out. He put the journal aside and wrung out his spare clothes. Everything was soaked. His sleeping bag alone weighed about twenty pounds. He sat on it, squeezing the water from it.

The day dragged on. His pack pulled him down with the wet weight until he couldn't walk any longer. He stopped earlier than usual and set up his tent, and he hung all of his clothes, including what he'd worn that day, on tree branches. As he slipped off his shorts, he laughed. He had stopped wearing underwear days before. He sat on a rock, his bare butt on the cool stone, and made a fire. He had become a real human, a person of the woods, as naked as the birds and squirrels. Except his shoulders were rubbed red from the pack he carried. Animals didn't need packs. The world was their pack.

He filled himself with pasta, granola bars, and beef jerky, and then he found two branches and used them to hold his clothes over the fire, drying them one piece at a time. When his clothes were dry, he read a little.

February 12th, 1935

We packed our final things today. We loaded our pickup high with furniture and packed the rest of our stuff in around it. As I write, Mother, Dad, and Grandad are riding in the cab, and I'm sitting atop all our possessions in the back, rocking back and forth as we roll down the road. I'm not certain where we're going. Grandad and Dad have been talking about some land east of Coal Creek.

It's strange leaving. Dad said we'll never come back here. The Big House will get torn down, and when the dam is closed, water will fill the land, fill it right up to the brim. Dad says the water will give us electricity, which we can use for all kinds of things. It's an odd concept. People sure are confused about what water is for. The preacher says it's for rebirth, Mother says it's for strengthening the soul, and Dad now says it's for electricity.

In any case, this'll be the last time I look at the north field, the Big House, the forests and bluffs. Maybe when the dam is closed, I'll come back and swim in the water. I'll look down into it and see, far beneath me, Grandad's tobacco rows.

February 27th, 1935

We got to the land Grandad leased and began settling into the new house. We've been here about a week. Our things were dusty from the road. Mother swept all the furniture off before

Dad and Grandad and I brought it into the house. It's smaller than our place on Grandad's farm in Coal Creek, but it's nicer. We have a toilet right in the house, right down the hall from where I sleep. I have my own room, unless Robert returns. Still, I don't really feel at home here. We don't know our neighbors. The landowner is a stranger. I hope Robert comes back. We haven't heard from him in a while. Dad sent him a few letters explaining what was happening in Coal Creek, but we've gotten no response.

Mother isn't feeling well, hasn't been since we left, really. Dad says she's just tired from the move. She's been in bed most of the week.

I've been exploring the new land some, when I'm not helping Grandad and Dad. There's lots of work to be done to prepare for planting season. This section of land hasn't been planted in a long time. It's full of weeds and thorns. Dad said that may be a good thing or bad thing. We can't know until the seeds are in the ground.

Eli slept well and began hiking early the following morning. His pace was slower than he anticipated because the forest was so thick, but that afternoon he made it to Watauga Lake, a giant man-made lake held in place by a dam built by the TVA. He sat on a rock. The water was calm and deep, a massive mirror reflecting the cloudless sky and forested hills. A sailboat drifted across it, shattering the image on its surface. Ripples spread out behind the boat and, after a glimmering moment, lapped against the shore. Eli ducked back into the woods. He needed to find a secluded area to camp. He would wake early the next morning, while it was still dark and hopefully before any boaters were out, and get back on the trail.

He tromped up a steep hill and stopped at the flattest spot he could find. The lake was visible beyond some thin trees, and across the water he could see the inside lip of the dam, a long bar of gravel with a road running over the top of it. Eli pitched his tent and ate granola bars and peanut butter, the last of the dried fruit, and some trail mix. He didn't want to risk drawing the attention of a park ranger or fisher by starting a fire. As he ate, he read his grandfather's journal.

March 5th, 1935

Mother is getting sicker. She hasn't been out of bed in over a week and she shivers beneath the covers. Dad and I went up to the landowner's house and called a doctor. They have their own telephone. I've never known someone who had one in their home. It seems like a silly thing to have in your house.

I met the landowner for the first time. His name is Mr. Rutherford, and he has several little children, but none near my age. It's a little lonely here. I miss Coal Creek, our neighbors, my friends. I hope Robert comes home soon.

March 7th, 1935

The doctor came today. He said Mother has malaria. He gave her some medicine, and Dad and I took turns wetting her forehead. She's got a bad fever that won't break. She can't hold any food down either. She looks frail, like a different person, and much older. I'm worried about her a lot. I haven't been sleeping well. I wake up with nightmares, afraid the Raven Mocker is coming for her. Last night, I sat next to her bed until morning, waiting and watching for him. Perhaps it's silly, but I think Mother appreciated it.

Her appearance has changed so quickly. She really is like a different person, like old age swept down on her in minutes rather than years. Her face is thin. She looks like she's about to sink away into the mattress, just disintegrate into sand.

March 11th, 1935

Mother died yesterday. I feel rotten inside, like the Raven Mocker climbed down my throat and is sitting inside me, polluting my spirit. It's not fair. Why couldn't the doctor fix her? Why couldn't I do something to help her? Why did we have to come here? Why did we leave Coal Creek?

We buried Mother in a clearing in the woods, just a few minutes from the house. Mr. Rutherford came down with his family and helped Grandad, Dad, and me carry the casket.

*We all stood in the woods. Mr. Rutherford's little children
held hands with their mother and each other. Dad stared at the
casket, motionless. He was like a statue of a man.*

Eli's watch woke him at four in the morning. He'd fallen
asleep before the sun went down and he felt rested. He pulled
his headlamp on and quickly packed his tent. He ate the last
two candy bars for breakfast as he walked down the hill and
followed the shore west. The image of his grandfather sitting
next to his mother's bed, waiting for the Raven Mocker to
come feed on her, hung in his mind.

The buzz of an engine frightened him. He ducked down
and turned off his headlamp. Headlights glowed through the
trees as the car passed on a road just a few yards up a hill to his
left. An early morning fisher, perhaps. He waited as the sound
faded away. Eli picked up his pace as he crossed an empty
parking area with a boat launch. He refilled his water from
a campground restroom on the west side of the lake. A few
tents were scattered among the trees. He crept past them.

The light on his head rocked with his steps. The lake was
to his right, the forest to his left. Eli had a sudden feeling
something stood among the trees, staring at him. He ignored
the woods, focusing instead on the water. The headlamp
cast a glimmering yellow beam on its surface. Eli heard a fish
splash far out and wondered what it had been hunting.

The forest pressed closer and closer to the water until Eli had no choice but to walk among the woods. They felt different than the woods he'd previously hiked through. Somehow, they felt fake, artificial, tainted in some way. Perhaps it was the man-made lake. Eli wasn't sure, but his imagination toyed with him. He was positive that at any moment he would feel a hand on his shoulder. He would turn and U`tlun'ta would cackle and stab him through the heart. He pulled his wrist rocket onto his arm, which made him feel a little safer.

His pace quickened. His pack bounced. The pot and spoon and food shuffled and banged together. Then the shore abruptly turned up, forcing Eli to climb a short hill, his boots slipping on gravel. Reaching the top, he saw the dam and a sign marking the Appalachian Trail.

He walked onto the dam. On one side of him the short lip he'd seen the previous day disappeared into the black water a few yards below. On the other side, however, the dam showed its true self. It sloped down for at least a hundred yards, massive steps built between two hills. It pressed against the lake, against all that water. All that water held back by a pile of rock and concrete. Eli imagined the dam crumbling away and the water gushing and flooding through the forest below. What would they find in the lake bed? Homes, perhaps, long destroyed by the rising water.

He loaded a stone in the sling and fired it off the dam. He lost sight of it almost immediately, but he waited and listened. A few seconds later he heard a soft noise as it landed.

Once off the dam, Eli followed the road for another minute or so, and then the white blazes led back into the woods. He walked on a high ridge, his headlamp fighting the darkness. He was thankful when the morning sun reached onto the ridgeline and lit the path.

With any luck, the forest rangers wouldn't be looking for him north of the lake. If he kept a steady pace, he would be out of Tennessee in another day or two. He passed a few other hikers around mid-morning. They said hello and continued on their way, chattering to each other. Under different circumstances, Eli would have liked to hike the trail with some friends. He liked spending time alone in the woods, but it was his ninth day on the trail, and the only people he'd said more than a few words to were Dalton and Hoary Jory. He wondered where Hoary Jory was. He was hiking north, just like Eli. Chances were pretty good they were only a few miles apart. If he did catch up with him, though, he supposed he wouldn't be able to talk to him. After all, Hoary Jory must have passed through the checkpoint a couple of days before. In fact, everyone on the trail who was walking north would probably have been informed to keep an eye out for Eli. Everyone, that is, who started hiking south of the checkpoint. He would have to be extra careful from then on out.

He looked off the trail, into the forest. "But you'll keep me out of sight, won't you?" He listened for a response from the trees or from the Yunwi Tsunsdi, but none came.

That evening, Eli hiked off the path and set up camp for the night. He gathered twigs for a fire and cooked some pasta as the sun set. Just before the sun slipped behind the horizon, light reached into the trees. The trunks turned gold on one side, shadow on the other. In the shadows the bark appeared dull, but in the light it glowed. As the sun dipped out of sight, the light on the bark tinted red. Deeper and deeper it grew, until the shadow reached around the trunks. The golden red faded to dull brown. The woods grew dark, twilight. But the light lingered and stayed with Eli. He would never forget that color.

Then the strum of a guitar tickled his ear. He held his spoon inches from his mouth, waiting to hear it again. A second later, music emanated from the trees. The Yunwi Tsunsdi were playing.

Eli grabbed his flashlight and followed the sound. It grew louder and voices joined in, the words lost in the distance. The twang of a banjo and whistle of a harmonica mixed with the woods. Eli felt the music around him. The sound lapped against his ears. It seemed to come from nowhere, from everywhere, spilling from the bark and the leaves. Then he saw a small fire and figures in shadow around it. He turned his flashlight off and leaned down. He snuck from tree to tree, closer and closer, and his heart danced with the music, quicker and quicker. He was about to see the Yunwi Tsunsdi.

Dee held a picture of Eli in one hand, her other hand absently petting Pepper, who sat in her lap. Eli should have crossed the checkpoint by then. They should have found him.

The wind whistled against the window. Dee looked at her reflection in the glass. The woods were dark. Dee couldn't imagine being out there alone. Her son was brave, she gave him that. Suddenly, her head rang with fear: if he was still alive.

Headlights broke her reflection, broke the thought. Pepper jumped off her lap. Dee put down the photo and stood up. As Susan walked up the porch holding a paper bag, Dee opened the door.

"I came over to fix you dinner," she said.

"I'm not really hungry, Susan."

Susan pushed inside. "Nonsense. You probably haven't eaten in days." She went straight for the kitchen. "Macaroni and cheese. Comfort food. That's what you need."

Dee sat down at the table and tried to smile but didn't really pull it off. "It's so dark out there."

Susan stopped unloading the grocery bag. "They just spotted him a few days ago, Dee. He'll turn up soon."

"That's what I keep wishing," Dee said, staring out the window.

The flames seemed to dance with the music. They created a bubble of light that pulsed, forcing its way into the darkness.

Eli could see a couple of figures in the shadow around the fire. He held his breath as one of them stood and approached the flames.

Eli's elation melted. It was a man, much too tall to be Yunwi Tsunsdi. The man threw some wood on the flames and sat back down. After a moment the fire started crackling and grew brighter, pushing the darkness farther into the forest. Eli saw there were several people gathered around it. One man was plucking a banjo, another blew into a harmonica, another tapped and fingered a guitar, and the rest of them sang. Behind them there was a shelter in the shadows.

Eli watched them for a while. They swayed together and clapped. One of the men jumped up and danced a little while the others laughed and cheered and whistled. Loneliness dropped into Eli's chest.

The music died down and the man with the banjo said something. Eli ducked behind a tree. Then the banjo picked up again and the clapping resumed. Eli slid down the trunk until he was sitting on the ground. Through the canopy, the stars coated the sky, millions and millions of them. He imagined his grandfather and father drifting among them.

Eli listened to a few more songs, each one making him more homesick and lonely than the last. Finally, when he felt tears fighting their way out, he walked back to his campsite and finished eating. His pasta had grown cold.

Eli reached Virginia on his tenth day in the woods. He stood on the border. A wooden sign read, "TENNESSEE/ VIRGINIA STATE LINE." The Jefferson National Forest spread to the north, the Cherokee National Forest to the south. The image of his mom, of his home, of the woods he knew so well, flickered behind his eyes. Eli briefly considered stopping where he was and returning to those woods and to his mom. Then he felt the pocketknife in his jeans. He would reach his goal. He would make his father proud. And he wouldn't remove his blindfold until morning.

Damascus was three and a half miles away. Eli would have to stop again. He still had plenty of oatmeal and pasta, but he'd burned through all his candy bars, granola bars, dried fruit, and almost all his trail mix. Though he dreaded going into town, dreaded leaving the trail and the security of the forest, he needed more food that didn't require a fire.

Eli walked into Damascus, a small town that catered to hikers and recreationists. Several old homes were scattered among the streets, mixed with bed and breakfasts, bike shops, stores, and churches.

Eli entered the first grocery store he saw. He walked through the aisles, plucking food from the shelves: dried fruit because it was lighter than canned, more granola bars, and trail mix. Though the food he really wanted was fresh meats and vegetables. He'd never felt hunger like that before. It was a grinding hunger, filled with cravings, compulsions. Unfortunately, the food his body told him to eat would spoil on the trail. As he shopped, his heart thumped. He was sure that any moment a forest ranger would walk in and grab him. He glanced at the clerk a few times, making sure she wasn't calling anyone.

He turned up an aisle lined with freezers: boxed dinners, bags of vegetables, frozen burritos piled behind frosty glass. He paused, looking at the food. His eyes shifted, refocused. Suddenly he was looking at himself, at his reflection. He was covered in dust and sweat. Spots of dry mud and blood speckled his shirt and grime coated his collar, pits, and chest. His hair was matted and frazzled. He ran his fingers through his hair, trying to fix his appearance, if only a little, and then he continued shopping.

When his basket contained as much as he could carry, he set the food on the counter. The clerk asked him if that would be it. Eli nodded. The clerk reached below the counter. Eli's calves tensed and his toes flexed in his shoes. He was ready to bolt if she picked up a phone. She pulled out a piece of paper—a flyer. Eli's nostrils flared and his breath stopped. He was going to have to run again.

"Methodist Church is having a hikers' lunch today," the clerk said, handing Eli the flyer.

Eli breathed.

"Free food. Info's on the paper." The clerk's accent was strange, foreign.

Eli thanked her and took the flyer. He had no intention of going. He just wanted to get the food and get back on the trail.

Back on the pavement, his shoulders relaxed. The grocery bags sank to his ankles and he loaded the food into his pack. It didn't look like much, but it weighed a lot. He glanced around for a garbage can to toss the flyer into but didn't see one. He didn't want to go back inside, so he just held onto it. He walked up the street.

The sidewalk seemed odd after days of walking on dirt. It was too flat, too perfect. It felt funny under his feet. Ignoring the paved path, Eli looked ahead of him. A few elderly men and women stood on the curb chatting with each other. After days of staring at trees, at leaves and ferns and grass, people seemed odd as well. They were oddly shaped. Their clothes, skin, eyes, nose, lips, and ears hung in the air, dangling as they spoke. They seemed to wobble all over as if their skin, their edges, drifted, drooped, and blurred into the space surrounding them. As Eli passed, he tried not to stare.

Not far up, he saw three hikers, two guys and a girl. They were staring at a telephone pole coated in staples and flyers.

One of the guys resembled a pear jammed on two toothpicks, with a face a child would have drawn. His mouth was just a line, his eyes too large, his nose seemingly one dimensional. The other guy was tall and comically thin. His bony arms made his shirt sleeves seem gigantic, and his legs were mostly knees. The girl with them moved and bounced, shifted her weight back and forth. Her head wobbled as she talked, as if she were a bobblehead doll. Her hands filled the space in front of her with gestures. She scrunched her fingers, pointed at her palm, threw both her hands in the air and let them fall to her side for a moment before she raised them again and started flinging them about.

Eli walked by them, not making eye contact. He just wanted to get on the trail and go, hike until night. But as he passed, the girl called out, "You know where that is?"

Eli stopped and turned. The three of them were looking at him. The pear on toothpicks crossed his arms. The stick man smacked his lips below a beak-like nose. The girl cocked her head to the side, and then straightened it, causing her ponytail to bounce and sway. Eli touched his chest.

The girl laughed. "Yes, you," she said, pointing at the flyer in his hand. "Do you know where that is? The hikers' luncheon? We just saw the same flyer on this pole and thought we'd go. But the stupid thing doesn't have directions on it. How are you supposed to find the church if you're not from here and they don't put directions on the flyer?" She spoke fast and her hair bounced with her words.

"I'm not sure where it is," Eli said.

"Well, come on, we'll find it together," the girl said. Eli looked at the pear on toothpicks and the comically thin guy. They were a little older than him. They didn't seem concerned that he was hiking alone.

"I'm not—I'm actually not going to the lunch," Eli said. "I'm heading back to the AT."

"And pass up a free meal?" the thin guy said. His nose wiggled when he spoke, almost as much as his Adam's apple, which poked cartoonishly from his neck. "You're crazy."

The other guy's chest, which was as big as a buffalo's, bounced with laughter.

Eli straightened the flyer. It had a picture of a barbecue sandwich on it. His mouth watered. He supposed that if he was with a group, no one would suspect he was a runaway. Unless, of course, they had a photo of him, like the clerk a few days before did. His stomach groaned. It was tired of candy bars, oatmeal, and pasta. "A free meal does sound good," Eli said.

The girl held out her hand. "My name's Magpie, well, my trail name's Magpie. My real name's Maggie. I like pie, blueberry especially, so Magpie. Get it?" she said.

"Yeah, and because you talk so much," the thin guy said. "Just like a magpie, always making noise."

Maggie let go of Eli's hand. She made a tiny fist and punched the boy in the arm. "This is Jimmy, goes by Jimbo out here. He's my brother's friend." She pointed at the boy the size of a buffalo, with arms as thick as a bear's legs. "That's my brother. We call him Willy Billy. His real name's Will. What's your trail name?"

Eli shook Jimmy's hand. He could feel his knuckles through his palm. "Tenneblind," he said, happy that he didn't have to give her his real name or make up a fake one. Thanks, Hoary Jory. Then he shook hands with Will. It was like shaking hands with a walrus. Eli's fingers were engulfed in flesh.

"Tenneblind," Maggie said. "Strange name, but I like it."

Will let Eli's hand go, and then he called to a woman crossing the street. "Do you know where the Methodist Church is?"

The woman pointed down the road. "Two blocks up and then left."

"Thanks," Will said, waving his thick and muscled forearm. "You old bag," he whispered.

Jimmy laughed. Maggie punched Will in the arm.

"What?" Will said. "I'm just joking."

"Well it's not funny," Maggie said.

Eli followed the three of them down the sidewalk, food the focus of his attention. In the background, Maggie spoke. "So how'd you get the name Tenneblind? It's a funky name. I like it."

"An old man gave it to me." Eli paused and then added, "I'm not sure why. He might have been crazy."

"Well we could give you a new one if you don't like Tenneblind. Or would that be bad luck? To change your name? I don't know. It might mess with your trail magic, you know, like karma. Is there such thing as trail karma? How far are you hiking? I'm going to be honest. You smell like a thru-hiker, no offense."

Eli laughed nervously. "I am. I'm going all the way to Maine."

"Yeah? All by yourself? Seems like a lot of time to spend by yourself. How long will that take? Did you start in Georgia? We met some folks earlier today who started in Georgia. We're only hiking the Virginia portion of the trail. Our mom is picking us up at the Maryland state line. We just started three days ago. We hiked up here from Warrensville. Haven't even gotten on the Appalachian Trail yet. This is Will's, excuse me, Willy Billy's second time to hike across Virginia. He did it last year with his dad. We have separate dads. I guess that only makes us half-siblings, technically, but we grew up together. Do you have any siblings?"

Eli wasn't sure if she was actually pausing to let him answer. After a second of silence, he said no, and she started right back in.

"That's too bad. Will's my only brother. Anyway, this year, Will's dad couldn't get the time off, but Will begged our mom to let him go anyway."

"I didn't beg her," Will said.

Maggie nodded her head at Eli and mouthed, "He did."

"This must be it," Jimmy said.

They stood in front of a church. Its doors were open and there were balloons tied to the handrail next to the steps. "Come on in, folks. You look hungry," a man in a suit and bolo tie said. "There's a place to drop your gear just inside."

They walked into a banquet hall with several foldout tables covered in plastic sheets. A dozen hikers mingled with old men and women. The smell of food and dusty books filled Eli's nose as his eyes adjusted to the interior light. The hikers wore tank tops and t-shirts, damp bandanas tied around their necks and heads, dry mud sticking to their weathered boots and legs. They looked odd seated next to men in gray suits and blue ties and women wearing pink dresses with lace collars and gold brooches shining in the halogens.

More tables lined the room and were filled with food. Salivating, Eli stared: piles of potatoes and rolls, dozens of cheesy casseroles and Crock-Pots full of steaming stews, plates of ketchup-covered meatloaf, fried chicken, glistening ribs. Maggie, Will, and Jimmy dropped their packs and leaned them against a wall.

Eli rubbed his hands together. Muck filled his nails. Sap and dirt stuck to his palms and arms.

"Better get you some food before your friends eat it all," a woman said, startling Eli. The vertical folds in her upper lip stretched apart as she smiled. Thin, clear hairs covered her chin, and her nostrils were as large and round as quarters. Her cheeks were cracked with age. It wasn't leathered skin that comes with sun exposure; it was skin aged in dim light—puffy, soft, and yellow-white. Empty hammocks hung under her eyes, and her gray hair framed her face. It might have been a wig. She wore a yellow dress that hung to her ankles, where thin brown socks, elastic long lost, sagged around wrinkled flesh.

Eli swallowed. He felt odd, or perhaps it was the room that felt odd around him. He didn't want to be there. He wanted to leave. He wanted to get back on the trail—but the food.

"Let me help you," someone said behind him.

Eli's pack lifted from his shoulders. The weight left him. He turned around. The man who'd welcomed them set Eli's pack next to Maggie's.

"Grab a plate," the man said, holding his hand toward the overflowing tables.

"Is there some place I might wash up?" Eli said. He held his hands up and then hid them, a little embarrassed.

The man laughed. "Of course." He led Eli down a carpeted hall that smelled like lavender and dust.

The bathroom door clicked closed and Eli flipped the lock. The sounds of the hikers and church people were muffled by the door. Eli took a breath and turned to the sink. He scrubbed the dirt away. The suds turned brown and splattered the porcelain. He squirted more soap into his palms, and he looked in the mirror. Soil and sweat smeared his forehead and his hair was a mess. He rinsed his hands and splashed water on his face. He rubbed at the dirt on his forehead, revealing the scars from the crash as if he was an archeologist dusting dinosaur bones from the earth. Muddy water dripped over the pink scars—relics that remained from a life that seemed unreal—from a face that seemed strange. But he was learning to accept this was his face. The scars weren't ugly, they just added a bit of texture to his skin. He focused on them, on the day it happened.

He had seen the church parking lot. The gray sedan. The driver's face. The images rolled through his mind. A flip-book of photos. One and then another and another. He touched his face. He touched the mirror. He saw the gray sedan in it. He saw his father's pickup. He saw himself in the passenger seat. He threw his hands up and yelled. The truck turned over. The bathroom seemed to roll with it. Eli braced himself on the sink and closed his eyes. He felt the room spinning, over and over. He opened his eyes. It wasn't the room that turned. He was back in the pickup, jostling around, strapped in with the belt. His father was next to him. Eli watched him slip from the seat and over the steering wheel as if he was as light as a doll. Then the sound of a thousand birds calling out at once split the air as his father hit the windshield and the glass broke around him—into him.

Eli closed his stinging eyes and slipped down the bathroom wall. His throat felt hot. Water dripped from his cheeks and onto his hands.

Someone knocked on the door. "Just a minute," Eli said, swallowing the image of the crash. He stood up. The brims of his eyes were red and swollen. He blew his nose and opened the door.

Jimmy was standing outside. "You all right in there? You going to move in or something?"

Eli walked past him without saying anything.

"It was just a joke," Jimmy called out to him.

Eli walked straight to his pack and picked it up.

Maggie ran over. "Hey, where are you going? You haven't even eaten yet."

Eli walked down the church steps and onto the sidewalk, ignoring Maggie behind him. He just wanted to be back in the woods, to keep walking. But then he saw a police car one block up. He stopped, wondered what to do. He had no idea. Running wasn't an option. He wouldn't make the woods. Hiding, too, was out of the question. He'd probably already been spotted.

"You're not even going to eat?" Maggie asked, standing on the sidewalk behind him. "I think I saw some blueberry pie in there."

The police car turned toward them and Eli spun around.

"I knew it," Maggie said. "No one can resist blueberry pie."

Had the cop seen him? He felt the pocketknife. He couldn't stop in Damascus. He couldn't let that happen.

"Come on," Maggie said. "A little food, a little pie, and then you can take off again. Heck, we could even hike together. Make our own trail magic."

The police car rolled by them. Eli controlled his breathing, contained his reflex to run.

"What's the matter?" Maggie asked.

As the police car kept going, Eli relaxed. He debated on turning for the trail again. But he figured if he was with a group of people it would be easier to avoid the rangers and police.

Maggie studied his face. His eyes must have betrayed him. "Have you been crying?"

Eli shook his head and stared into the field next to the church. Past the field, a grove of trees moved in the wind, shaking their leaves. He had no words. He had so much to say and no words would do.

"It seems like you could use some company," Maggie said.

Eli watched the branches blowing in the wind. Their motion made him feel static.

"Everyone could use some company." Maggie looked at her feet. "Will and Jimmy can be a couple blockheads sometimes, and I know I talk a little too much, but hiking with us isn't so bad."

Eli looked at her. From the corner of his eye, he could still see the leaves.

"Okay, I talk a lot too much," Maggie laughed. "Sorry about that. I can't help it."

Eli found himself laughing with her. It surprised him. It wasn't what she said. It was the situation; the whole situation suddenly became clear to him. There he was, a person on a planet in a giant galaxy of stars. He was a speck of dust and nothing more. And there was this other speck of dust talking to him, and she was apologizing for it. Eli couldn't help himself. Life was absurd. It was laugh-out-loud absurd. So that's what he did. He laughed genuinely for the first time in months, the first time since his father died. It felt good. He wiped his eyes, tears of laughter mixed with tears of sorrow.

Their laughter settled around them. Eli glanced back into the field, at the trees. The limbs and leaves were still.

"Come on," Maggie said.

Eli followed her back to the church, and she filled the silence.

"So how'd you get those scratches on your face, anyhow? And how old is that pack? It looks a hundred years old."

Eli devoured his food, and topped the meal off with a piece of pie. After they ate, Will and Jimmy made a paper football and were flicking it back and forth. Jimmy kept yelling "Boom!" every time the football passed through Will's thick-fingered goalposts, which happened often. Maggie chatted with the woman next to her. Eli listened while he ate the pie. Maggie told the woman all about hiking, the animals scurrying about, the beautiful trees, a rain storm.

Eli scraped the whipped cream off his plate and debated on having another slice. He didn't think his stomach could handle it, though.

Maggie leaned toward her brother. "He's going to join us on the trail," she said nodding to Eli.

Will raised his eyebrows at her. "Really? You just decided that on your own?" He flicked the paper football at Jimmy.

"What's the big deal, Will?"

"The big deal is that since we started, you've been trying to set our schedule and make all the decisions. And now you're inviting strangers to hike with us?"

Eli cleared his throat. "It's fine. I can hike on my own."

Maggie shook her head. "There's no need. We're all going the same direction." She glared at Will. "Will's always like this, always has to be the big man in charge, telling everyone what to do."

"Shut up, Maggie," Will said, holding his fingers up as goal posts.

"I will if you tell me why we wouldn't join up. Wasn't it you who talked so much about the magic on the trail? And the people you meet? And the names you give each other?"

Will rolled his eyes. "Fine. Whatever you want, Princess Magpie."

The man who'd taken Eli's pack from his shoulders stepped onto a chair at the far end of the room. His bolo tie bounced on his chest and he held a Bible.

"Excuse me, everyone." A dozen dirty hikers glanced up from paper plates piled with ribs and chicken. The man continued, "Following the meal, we're going to have some singing and a sermon in the auditorium. I'd like to invite all of you to rest a little longer, fill your bellies, and then join us."

Jimmy flicked the paper football through Will's fingers. "Boom!"

Maggie shot him a nasty look.

"I like your enthusiasm, young man," the man in the bolo tie said, pointing at Jimmy. A few of the church people laughed, the hikers went back to eating, and the bolo tie stepped down from the chair.

Maggie leaned over Eli and punched Jimmy in the arm. "That was rude, Jimmy," she said, half whispering.

Will flicked the paper football back to Jimmy.

"Sorry, Magpie," Jimmy said. He propped up the paper football with one finger and made his hand into a little man, with fingers for legs. He ran down the table and flicked the football. It flew through Will's goalposts. "Boom!"

Maggie looked at Eli. "What do you think? Should we stay?" Before Eli could think about it, Maggie glanced behind her, ensuring none of the church goers were too close, and then she leaned, conspiratorially, toward Eli. "I don't really want to. I'm not much for sermons, though I do like to sing. Camp songs mostly. But I'd like to get going. Is that rude, though? To just eat and leave?"

"They can't make us stay," Will said, propping up the paper football.

Jimmy mimicked a cheerleader. "Rah, rah, rah! Gooooooo, Will!"

Will laughed and shook his head at Jimmy. "You're stupid," he said, flicking the football, which flew across the table, wide right, and hit Jimmy in the arm.

"You blew," Jimmy said.

Across the room, a few other hikers tossed their paper plates in the trash and hoisted their packs onto their shoulders. The bolo tie walked over to them. "Got to get back on it, huh?" he said.

Maggie turned back to the group. "Let's just stay for a bit," she said. "It's rude not to. We'll just sing a song or two and then go."

Eli wanted to get back on the trail. He'd lost enough time already. He wasn't sure what to do. He could leave, but the police and Forest Service were looking for a lone hiker. His best bet of getting out of Damascus and back on the path was probably with a group. Staying with Maggie, her brother Will, and Jimmy increased his chances of remaining unrecognized. But they didn't seem to be in much of a hurry, so staying with them might considerably slow his pace. That, and Will didn't seem happy to have Eli joining them. Still, he supposed if he stayed with them just for a day, until he was out of Damascus and back in the woods, then he could leave them on the trail, set out early the next morning, like Hoary Jory had done. He could make up mileage later. At least that way, he could ensure he didn't walk through the town's streets alone to be seen and picked up by the police.

"I'd vote we get back on the trail," Eli said. "But if you think we should stay, then I don't mind."

"We're staying," Will said.

Maggie looked at Will, then at Eli. "I told you. He always has to be the one to make the decisions."

The bolo tie opened the door to the auditorium and started singing, gently waving his hands, calling everyone in. The other church people joined in the singing. A few more hikers picked up their packs and headed for the door. Others tossed their plates and walked into the auditorium. Maggie, Will, and Jimmy all looked at each other. Jimmy flicked the paper football, Will shrugged, and Maggie stood up and walked toward the bolo tie.

Eli, Jimmy, and Will followed her. The voices of several dozen people filled the small auditorium. Maggie, Will, and Jimmy sat down in a pew near the rear of the room. Eli sat next to them. The woman wearing the yellow dress pushed in beside him. She smiled at Eli, exposing tiny gray teeth. Peach fuzz coated her chin. Her eyes were small and wrinkled. She rocked back and forth and patted Eli's leg. Eli shifted in the pew, tried to scooch away from her.

A few men in ties filed into the pew in front of them. They sang deeply. Eli could almost feel the vibration of their voices. It buzzed in the wood beneath him.

Eli didn't know the lyrics, but Maggie jumped right into the singing, though she didn't seem to know all the lyrics either. Eli smiled and watched her. He was trying to keep his mind off the old woman beside him.

The song ended and the bolo tie asked them to open their songbooks to another page. Will and Jimmy each took a book from the back of the pew in front of them. The woman in the yellow dress leaned closer to Eli, offering to share her book. The sound of the song echoed off the wooden ceiling and walls. Eli hummed and mumbled along with the music. The woman put her arm around him and rocked them back and forth. Eli swallowed and sweated. He glanced at Maggie, who smiled at him, on the verge of laughing.

Then Jimmy mouthed the words "so sweet." He put his arm around Will and mimicked Eli and the old woman. Will shook Jimmy off.

The song ended and another started. The woman continued to rock side to side with her arm around Eli, and Jimmy made kissing faces at him. Maggie saw it and slapped Jimmy on the leg. He stopped for a moment.

The singing continued, the noise bouncing around inside the auditorium, bouncing around inside Eli's head. He swayed with the woman in the yellow dress, mumbling lyrics deep in his throat. He felt the knife in his pocket. What was he doing there? He should be on the trail, not sitting around singing. He felt hot. The room seemed to grow very small. The grain of the wood on the pews and floor appeared fake. Eli lifted his head. It felt heavy. He couldn't tell where the ceiling began and where the walls ended. Everything blended together as if it were carved continuously from the same tree. And the singing dripped over it all. He was vaguely aware of his arm rising and wiping sweat from his forehead. The woman's arm around him seemed to weigh a hundred pounds. It seemed to smash him down and the swaying suddenly felt like shaking.

Then the arm slipped from his shoulder. Eli stopped swaying and looked at the woman's skin. It seemed odd, textured like stone. Her hand extended to flip the songbook's page. Her fingers were folded into a tiny fist. She held something. Eli thought it was a tissue at first, but then black liquid, like mud, dribbled between her fingers. Before Eli could react to the liquid, he saw her forefinger. He saw it clearer than he'd ever seen anything. The woman's first finger was long and sharp.

Eli's heart slipped, sank, splashed into his stomach. He stared at the woman. Her face was chiseled from rock. She winked at him and smiled, her lips wrinkled, her gums recessed, her teeth rotted.

Eli stood and pushed past Jimmy, Will, and Maggie. He rushed through the auditorium doors and passed the tables filled with food. He stepped into the light of day. He held his ground as the world spun around him.

Then he vomited in the grass. The singing quieted as the doors of the church closed behind him. He wiped the spit from his lips and his heart slowed. He couldn't have seen that. He couldn't have really seen—been sitting next to—U`tlun'ta.

Eli sat on the church steps, staring at a trail of ants carrying bits of food across the sidewalk. They'd find his vomit soon. They'd cut it up and carry it down into their nest.

Will, Jimmy, and Maggie came out of the church. Maggie set Eli's pack next to him. "Don't forget that," she said.

Eli squinted up at her. The sun framed her head and cast her shadow over him. Gold speckled her eyes. Curls of hair messily hung in her face.

"We're going to get on the trail," she said. "Again, you're welcome to hike along with us. Will said we can make Saunders Shelter by night. That way we don't have to set up tents. Have you been sleeping in shelters or a tent? We've been in tents since we left Warrensville."

Eli put on his pack. "I've done a little of both."

"Aw, sick," Jimmy said. "Somebody yacked over here." He was standing on the sidewalk looking at the grass where Eli puked.

As they left Damascus, birds flew overhead, wings open, feet tucked, drifting and hunting. Eli watched them as he walked. His mind wandered into the sky. He could almost feel the sun on his wings. Then he bumped into Maggie. She turned around and smiled at him. He apologized and focused on the path.

They hiked all afternoon. Will was the pace setter. Eli brought up the rear. Maggie walked in front of him. She jabbered away for the first mile or so, asking dozens of questions and leaving him no space to respond, but by the second mile they all were mostly silent.

It was strange to be with other people, to walk with other people, after miles and miles spent alone. It changed Eli's rhythm. When walking alone, he'd paid more attention to the trees, the birds, the insects. He built his pace around the trail, around his own thoughts. He was able to wander and wonder through his mind. But with the group he had to adjust his tempo to the person in front of him. It moved his focus away from the forest and his muse. He focused more on keeping pace, adjusting as the group slowed and quickened to suit the terrain. The pace was slower than his usual pace, too.

They made it to Saunders Shelter about six hours later. Will and Maggie collected wood for a fire and Eli and Jimmy fetched some water.

"So you're hiking all the way to Maine?" Jimmy asked as they walked down the path.

"Yep," Eli said.

"Pretty far. I don't know if I'd like to do that alone."

Eli touched the pocketknife. He wanted to say he wasn't alone, that his grandfather and father were with him. Instead, he just kept quiet.

At the stream, Jimmy filled his canteen and took a swig of the water.

Eli's jaw dropped. "You need to boil that," he said.

Jimmy looked at the water. "Why?"

"Raw water like this can carry all kinds of nasty stuff in it, bacteria and things. You could get sick."

Jimmy shrugged and poured the water out of his canteen.

They sat around the fire. Maggie sang softly, songs Eli had never heard. Will and Jimmy poked at the coals and played with the flames, tossing leaves and twigs into it. It had been a long day. Eli felt the wound on his leg—a long several days. He tilted his head back and breathed out. The stars glimmered through the trees. The universe was a big place, the Earth just a tiny dot, drifting half in darkness, half in light. And he was just a tiny speck standing on its surface. Suddenly, the idea that his father and grandfather were with him seemed silly. They were dead, and he was alone on the AT—almost alone.

He looked at Will and Jimmy, at Maggie. The flames whittled away at the wood, casting dancing shadows on her face. Behind her, the forest bared its dark teeth at Eli. For the briefest moment, just a microsecond, he saw

U`tlun'ta walking through the woods, her arm raised, her sharpened finger pointing. But then there were only trees. He swallowed and focused on the flames.

Things always seemed different at night; thoughts that once were clear and sharp became dappled with doubt. Maybe he wouldn't leave early in the morning after all. It was nice to not be alone, especially at night.

The following morning, Eli ate oatmeal for breakfast. In the morning light, with his nighttime fears shed, the comforting company of others didn't seem so poignant. He debated once again whether or not he should stay with the group. It was nice the previous night, being with other people when the woods were dark. But hiking with other people meant a slower pace. He didn't know what to do. He touched the knife in his pocket. And then Maggie sat down in front of him and smiled. Eli brushed his hair back and swallowed a bite of oatmeal.

Maggie peeled an orange. "I love oranges, don't you?"

Eli nodded. "I do."

"Kiwis may be my favorite, though," she said. "Kiwis or pineapple. I love pineapple, and regular apples. Bananas, those are good too. And cherries."

"So basically, you like all fruit," Eli said.

"I guess so." Maggie laughed.

Their eyes connected for a second, a second that seemed to turn over for an hour, a second that made up his mind about staying with the group, a second Eli knew he'd come back to all day long as he hiked with them.

Then Jimmy sat down next to Maggie. "You are a fruit," he said around a mouthful of banana. He tossed the peel over his shoulder. It landed in the brush and scared two sparrows into the trees.

Eli watched the birds for a moment and then turned back to Maggie. He smiled, but she didn't look at him. She punched Jimmy in the arm.

"Ouch," Jimmy said.

"If your arms weren't so thin it wouldn't hurt," Maggie said.

"Ouch again, Magpie," Jimmy said.

Eli stood. "Well, should we go? Everybody ready?"

Will raised his eyebrows at Eli. "Hold your horses there, boss," he said. He sat on the ground, his back against the shelter's wall, his legs crossed on his pack, a guidebook in his thick fingers.

Eli leaned against the picnic table. Clearly, Will wanted to be in charge. Eli didn't mind that. Will was four years older than him. Eli just didn't want to waste time waiting when he could be making miles.

Jimmy opened a granola bar. "You think we could catch one of those little birds?" he said to Maggie.

"What little birds?" Maggie asked.

Jimmy pointed. One of the sparrows stood on a tree branch, twitching its head from side to side.

"It would be pretty difficult," Eli said.

Jimmy broke off a piece of his granola bar and tossed it underneath the tree. The sparrow looked around and then dived to the ground. It pecked at the chunk of granola.

"I think it's too big," Maggie said.

Eli watched the bird. It twitched its head back and forth, snatching bits off the granola with its beak. Was this a skin-walker, Eli wondered. A man turned bird? A bit of his grandfather's magic?

Jimmy stood up. He slipped from the picnic table and approached the bird, stalking. Before he took three steps, the bird darted back up into the trees. Jimmy feigned sadness and sat back down.

"Nice try," Maggie said, popping a piece of orange in her mouth.

"Okay," Will said from the ground. "Let's go."

With their stomachs satisfied for the moment, they shouldered their packs and set out again. Eli tried to take the lead. He wanted to set the pace a little faster than the day before, but Will stepped in front of him. Eli relinquished and fell to the rear of the pack.

Their initial pace was good, though. Eli figured they would cover about three miles an hour if they kept it up, but they didn't. Shortly after they began, the trail swooped down into a gap and then shot up. Maggie, Jimmy, and Will were puffing before they reached the crest. When they finally did, Will sat down on a rock.

"We're breaking already?" Eli asked. It had been less than an hour.

"We're just drinking some water," Will said. "You can keep going."

Eli looked down the trail. The woods crept toward it. A titmouse sang in the distance. The woman from the church, her leathered skin and yellowed teeth, crept into his mind. He pictured the pew they'd sat on, saw it in the woods. It was covered in lichens and moss and mold, vines curled around its legs. He saw himself sitting on it, while the titmouse called again and again. Behind him, U`tlun'ta slithered through the ferns. She reached out to him, her fingers tucked into a fist, holding something that leaked black liquid. Only her spear-finger, made of sharpened bone, extended toward him. Just before she touched his shoulder, Eli blinked the vision away.

He turned to Maggie. A breeze played in her hair. "No, it's okay," Eli said. "I'll wait."

Dee called Ben's office. His phone rang several times and then went to voicemail. She swallowed. "Ben, it's Dee." She tapped her fingers on the table. "I ..." She didn't know what to say. She wanted to scream, to yell, "Where's my son?" She wanted to smash the phone. Instead, she said, "Ben, call me back and let me know how the search is going." She hung up and slid the phone down the table.

She stood up and paced. She didn't know what else to do. She just paced until the phone rang. She snatched it from the table. "Hello?"

"Hey, Dee," Ben said. "I just got your message."

"And?"

"We're doing all we can to find him. He didn't pass the checkpoint, so the rangers are looking south of there, and they searched the woods near the store where he was spotted. I don't know what to tell you. They're looking for him. I'm sorry we haven't found him yet."

Dee only nodded. She felt like exploding.

That afternoon, Jimmy fell behind. Maggie and Eli stopped to wait for him as Will pressed forward. "Hey," Maggie called up the trail to Will. "Wait for a minute."

Will stopped and came back to the group. Jimmy was unlacing one of his boots. "What's the matter?" Will asked.

"My feet are killing me," Jimmy said. He pulled off his boot and rolled off his sock, which had imprinted his sweaty ankle. His heel was swollen with a blister. "Gross," Jimmy said.

"Are they both like that?" Eli asked.

"They both hurt." Jimmy unlaced his other boot. The back of his other foot was just as bad.

Eli set his pack down and took the moleskin from his first aid kit. He patched Jimmy's boots with it and then gave Jimmy two large Band-Aids. "Cover the blisters with these."

The rest of the day, their pace was slow. Jimmy stopped several times and let his feet rest. Eli began to get a little discouraged. At their rate, it would take him a year to get to Maine. He felt the pocketknife, and he recalled the look Maggie had given him that morning. There were implications in that look, Eli thought. Implications he couldn't completely foresee, but he could feel them, like a leaf plucked from the branch by wind. The leaf couldn't know where the wind would take it; it could only know that it was caught in something larger than itself.

That night, Will and Jimmy went to get water.

Eli and Maggie collected some twigs to start a fire. They tossed their collected kindling in a pile. Eli swallowed. "So how do you guys know Jimmy?"

"Oh, he's been a friend of Will's since they were little," Maggie said, pushing the hair out of her eyes. "I swear, my brother and Jimmy didn't go anywhere without each other until they were in high school."

Eli stacked some twigs on a bit of paper, and then he lit the paper on fire. He blew the flame onto the wood. It smoked and then caught as the paper curled into ash. "You and Will grew up together, though, right?"

"Yeah, we have different dads, but Will's dad isn't around much. My dad sort of raised him. It's only been in the last few years that Will's dad has come around."

Eli set some more twigs on the fire. It began to pick up. "So you and Jimmy are kind of like siblings then, huh?" Eli snatched a glance of Maggie and then looked back at the fire. "I mean, if he and Will have been hanging out since they were little, and since you're a few years younger than Will, it must be like you had two brothers."

Maggie crouched down next to the tiny fire. "I never thought of it like that. I guess so, though. I mean, I've known Jimmy since before kindergarten."

Eli smiled at the fire.

The following day, Jimmy's blisters popped, and the group stopped so that he could use some of Eli's antibacterial cream and re-bandage his heels. Eli kneeled down and dug the items out of his bag.

"Thanks for giving me these," Jimmy said as he pulled off his boots.

"We'll pick up a first aid kit in the next town," Will said, standing behind Eli. "Sorry I forgot to bring one."

"It's a good thing I asked Eli to hike with us then," Maggie said.

"It's no problem," Eli said, looking at Jimmy. "I know how it feels."

Jimmy's pace picked up that afternoon, and they settled into camp for the night, out of breath and sore-shouldered.

Eli dropped his pack and started gathering twigs. He glanced at Jimmy and Will, waiting for them to go fetch water. Jimmy sat down and started unlacing his boots. Maggie shook her head at Will. "I'm on kindling duty tonight."

Will turned to Eli. "Fetch some water?"

Eli glanced at Jimmy's feet. He wanted a chance to talk to Maggie alone a little more, but Jimmy couldn't be expected to walk more than necessary. Eli nodded his head and stood.

As they filled the pots to the brim in a spring nearby, Will said, "Fourteen and hiking the AT alone, huh?"

Eli nodded. He tried not to show his worry. He'd thought hiking with other teenagers would keep him off the radar of any adults they passed. But it seemed he may have just fallen directly onto Will's radar.

"Tenneblind. It's not a bad trail name for someone from Tennessee, I suppose."

Eli wasn't sure what to say, wasn't sure if Will knew he was a runaway. "Willy Billy—it's good too." Eli wanted to turn the conversation away from himself. "Did your father give you that name?"

"He did," Will said. "Last year when I hiked Virginia with him."

Eli stood, steadying his pot so he wouldn't splash water from it. "You must miss him."

Will seemed to swell and anger slid down his face. "What do you know?"

Eli almost told Will about his own dad, about how much he missed him, but the words didn't take form. "Nothing," Eli said. "I just—Maggie mentioned that you didn't really know your father growing up."

"Well Maggie talks too much," Will said, shaking his head. He headed back to the shelter, water sloshing from the pot onto his boots.

"I'm sorry," Eli said, following him up the trail.

Each day seemed to begin the same, and Eli fell into a rhythm again, although it was different with other people involved. They chatted about the woods, the trail, the birds, and Eli joked about trail magic with Maggie.

She hiked hard. When they hit steep climbs, even when Eli began to feel the burn of needles in his lungs and his face pulled into a grimace, she managed to smile as she fought for breath. The group as a whole did pretty well. Will continued to set the pace, and Eli followed, listening to the birds and Maggie chatter. When he could get a word in, he talked to her, and he also talked to Jimmy, but Will didn't say much to him.

During the day Eli would have liked to set his own pace. He could have covered many more miles on his own. But during the night, when even the insects were silent, Eli was glad to have people around him.

One such night, when the woods seemed especially dark, Will and Jimmy both walked away from camp carrying a roll of toilet paper, their flashlights swinging at their sides. Maggie and Eli were alone again. The fire crackled in front of them. Maggie hugged her knees to her chest and rested her head on her arm. The yellow flames winked in her eyes.

Eli swallowed. He felt something trying to escape his mouth. His tongue convulsed with it, and his lips parted, but nothing came out. He tossed a twig on the coals. Yellow and blue flame burst from it, gliding along its surface, devouring the wood. Then the flames on it dwindled, and the twig slowly turned into an orange ember, holding its shape—in fact, clinging to its original form until the last minute, when it glowed brightest and then broke into pieces. Eli opened his mouth again, but before anything came out, Maggie spoke.

"Tenneblind," she said, staring into the flames, not really speaking to Eli, but seeming to just say the word, feel it in her mouth, feel it in the air. Then she looked up at Eli.

Eli smiled and held her gaze. He tried not to blink for fear that in that dark instant Maggie would look away. He feared that if he closed his eyes Maggie would be gone when he opened them. He would wake and realize that he only dreamed he was hiking with her.

"What's your real name?" Maggie asked.

"Eli Jack." Half real, half fake. The hybrid had come from nowhere. The words had just filled his mouth, like water rushing into a cup and over the brim. They spilled out before Eli could shut off the faucet. He hadn't intended to lie to her. In a way, it wasn't a lie, Eli supposed. True, his birth name wasn't Eli Jack, but he didn't feel that it was a lie to call himself that. His name was Eli Jack as much as it was Tenneblind.

"It's a good name," Maggie said. "Eli Jack." Again, she spoke as if to hear it herself more than to speak to Eli.

Eli wanted to move around the fire, wanted to sit next to Maggie, to put his arm around her, to touch her hair, her lips—

A high-pitch scream broke his thoughts and straightened his spine. His eyes left Maggie, shot up behind her. Maggie turned and stared into the woods as well. Only darkness was there.

Maggie turned back to Eli. "What was that? Do you think Will and Jimmy are okay?"

Eli shook his head. Before he could answer, the sound of Will laughing came from the trees, followed by the pendulum swing of flashlight beams. Will and Jimmy walked back into the camp, laughing.

"What's so funny?" Maggie asked. "What was that sound?"

"Jimmy tripped over a log," Will said, chuckling. "You should have seen it. Classic Jimmy. Fell right on his face. Screamed like a little girl." Will's chest and shoulders bounced with laughter.

"You all right, Jimmy?" Maggie asked.

Jimmy shined his flashlight on his limbs, inspecting them, and smiled at Maggie. "Looks like it."

Eli tossed another twig in the flames.

After a few days, their food supplies dwindled. Will read his guidebook. There wasn't a proper grocery store for quite a ways, but there was a small trail stop not far away. When they reached it, a closed sign was propped in the window.

Eli pressed his face against the glass. A few shelves of food stood in the dim building. He had perhaps another day's worth of meals on him. He wasn't sure how much the others had. On the side of the building, there were two vending machines.

Eli took out his money and started feeding dollars into one machine. Will did the same on the other. They bought a dozen sodas and sat at a picnic table. They each guzzled one down, their mouths fizzing with carbonation. Then Jimmy let out a roaring burp.

"Gross!" Maggie said, though she laughed.

Will laid down in the shade of a tree and closed his eyes. Eli opened another soda and took out his grandfather's journal.

March 20th, 1935

Dad hasn't said anything in days. He's been sitting by the window, staring at nothing. Time is slipping by, slipping over me in the strangest way. It seems diluted, like a drop of blood in water. At first it holds its shape, stays close together, but then it spreads out, thins until you can't see it anymore. I can't feel the time passing anymore. I'm stuck in this moment, Dad staring out the window, Grandad working in the field. It feels like this will last forever.

I can't take it any longer. I need to get away from here.

Eli had read that journal entry a dozen times. He felt like his grandfather was speaking directly to him. In the days after his father died, he'd spent most of his time running through the woods, running until his legs wobbled and his chest and guts felt like bursting. Life wasn't fair sometimes, but somehow, reading about his grandfather's loss helped.

It was the shared experience. Even if that sharing happened across time, it still helped.

Eli took a sip of the soda. It was so sweet. His body buzzed with energy. The others must have felt the same way. Their mighty chief had only laid down for a few minutes when he stood up and led them back to the trail.

For a few miles, Will set the pace significantly faster than usual, but by mid-afternoon, they were dragging again. The caffeine and sugar was all burned up.

Luckily, the trail wasn't too difficult. It led onto a narrow dirt road. On one side the forest was thick, on the other, thin. It had probably been cleared several years before for farmland. Eli could see an old fence in the distance.

Maggie stopped walking. She wiped sweat from her face and drank some water. "I need a break, Will."

Will turned. "We just stopped."

"That was hours ago," Maggie said.

Will glanced at his watch. "We need to keep going if we're going to make the next shelter before dark."

Maggie sat down and blew the hair from her face. "Keep going then. I'll catch up. But right now, I'm taking a break."

Jimmy sat down next to her. "It's hot, Will. I'm sure we'll make it. Ten minutes isn't going to make a difference."

Will nodded his head and shrugged off his pack. "It is damn hot out here."

Eli was tired and hungry, but he also wanted to keep going, to push through. He stood on the road for a minute and then let his pack slide off his back as well. In the distance, the fence leaned. At some point, it had probably held cattle or horses in place, but it had become nothing more than a couple of rusted wires clinging to rotting posts. Around the fence, the trees were motionless, the grass still as death.

Then Eli saw something move beyond the old fence. He saw it only momentarily. It darted through tall grass. He scanned the woods—nothing. He looked back to where Maggie, Will, and Jimmy sat. Out of the corner of his eye, he saw it again. It moved between two trees. "There's something over there," he said.

"Squirrel?" Jimmy asked without moving.

"No, bigger." Eli waited to see it again.

"Fox?" Jimmy said.

"Possibly. I think it might be bigger than that, though." Eli surveyed the forest. Something rattled the brush to his left. "There it is." He turned, but it was already out of sight again. He listened—silence. He watched—stillness. Perhaps it was the Yunwi Tsunsdi playing with him.

Maggie came over. She squinted. "Let's go see what it is," she said, and then called to Will and Jimmy, "Come on."

"Now you want to go?" Will asked.

"Don't be a jerk, Will," Maggie said. She walked off the road.

"I'm not going," Will said.

"That's fine," Maggie said, imitating his tone.

Jimmy shrugged at Eli, as if to say, "What's new? They've been bickering since Maggie was three." Then Jimmy stood up and followed Maggie.

Eli tromped through the brush behind him. A few surprised birds fluttered into nearby trees. The three of them reached the old fence. Beyond it, a short hill sloped into what seemed like miles of bushes speckled with bright red berries.

"Oh my goodness," Maggie said. "That's beautiful."

"You think those are edible?" Jimmy asked. "They look a little like raspberries." He carefully climbed over the fence, avoiding the rusted barbs, and walked down into the bushes. He pulled a berry off the plant and popped it in his mouth. "It's delicious!"

"There's a bunch of berries over here, Will!" Maggie yelled behind them.

Eli turned to the road. Tall grass obscured his view. He couldn't see Will.

Maggie shrugged. "Whatever."

Eli held the wire up so Maggie could slip under it. She did the same for him. They trotted down the hill and followed Jimmy into the bushes. Eli picked a berry the size of his thumb and stuck it in his mouth. It was possibly the best thing he'd ever eaten. It was so sweet. It made the soda he'd drunk taste like water. He grabbed more. The fat little berries burst on his tongue, and his fingers turned red from the juice. "This must be leftover from an old farm," he said.

"Maybe it used to be an old winery or something."

"Winery?" Maggie asked. She wiped red juice off her chin. Her mouth and hands were full of berries.

"Yeah, during prohibition," Eli said, "there were lots of farmers out here who made more money selling alcohol than they did vegetables." Eli stuffed more berries in his mouth.

Then something moved through the brush behind Maggie. Eli turned and saw a man staring at him. A stringy white beard hung to the man's waist. His skin was leathered and old, his eyes cracked and red. The crow's feet at their corners crept down his cheeks and disappeared beneath his beard. Eli froze. Something about the man terrified him. It was like his face was a mask. Eli almost expected the man to reach up and remove it.

Maggie followed Eli's gaze over her shoulder. She stopped picking berries and stared at the man.

Farther into the field, Jimmy kept eating, stuffing the berries into his mouth.

"Jimmy," Maggie whispered.

He kept at the berries, grabbing them by the handful.

"Jimmy!" she said again.

Jimmy's head shot up. "What?" he said. He glanced at Maggie and Eli, who both stood still. He turned to the man. At the sight of him, Jimmy dropped the berries in his hand.

Maggie, Eli, and Jimmy all swallowed, their mouths red with juice, their lips and hands stained with guilt.

Then the man screamed, a sound like nothing Eli had ever heard before, a rasping, throaty, primitive noise that filled the woods.

They needed no other prompt. All three of them bolted through the berry bushes toward the fence. The bushes shook around them, scratching their legs and arms and scattering berries beneath their feet.

Eli scrambled up the hill and made it to the fence first. He held the wire up. Maggie slipped underneath it. Jimmy was a little ways behind. He was sprinting toward the hill but tripped over a rock. He fell hard on his chest. Behind him, a fox darted through the bushes.

Eli glanced at Maggie. She was heading toward the road, legs pumping. He turned back to Jimmy. A low moan rolled from his mouth as he turned onto his side. His eyes pinched in pain as he held his chest. Eli shuffled down the hill and ran to him. "Come on, Jimmy," Eli said, pulling him to his feet.

Jimmy pushed himself up, and they headed for the fence. Eli helped him up the hill and then through the fence. On the other side, Jimmy held the wire for Eli while pressing his free hand into his chest. His breath sounded shallow as he sucked in air. Then they ran toward the road. Eli chanced a glance over his shoulder. The old man stood at the top of the hill and stared at them.

When they reached the road, Eli turned around, panting. The man was gone.

Jimmy was limping and his leg bled, his chest heaved with irregular breath, but they didn't stop. Maggie already had her pack on. Eli and Jimmy grabbed theirs as well.

"What's going on?" Will said.

Maggie and Eli looked at each other, eyes wide.

"What happened to him?" Will pointed at Jimmy.

"No idea," Maggie said. "Let's just go."

"Hold up! What's going—"

"Let's just go!" Maggie yelled at Will. She started walking up the road.

Eli turned to Will. "I think he just got the wind knocked out of him. He fell," Eli said. "But I really do think we should go." He turned and followed Maggie. Jimmy did the same, though he coughed and groaned.

They hiked in silence for a bit. Maggie led the way, followed by Eli, followed by Jimmy, and then Will. Then Maggie stopped at the top of a hill and sat down.

"Are you going to be okay?" she asked Jimmy. "You're bleeding."

A few long, zigzagging scratches bled down his ankle. Jimmy took a few deep breaths and then said, "I'm fine. Just fell on some rocks."

"What happened back there?" Will asked.

Maggie blew the hair out of her face. "Some freak in the woods. You didn't hear him screaming?"

Will shook his head. "I didn't hear anything. All I know is that you guys came running out of the woods like it was on fire, and Jimmy's moaning like a whale." Will laughed a little.

Jimmy joined him. "Felt like someone stomped on my chest. I couldn't get any air." He rubbed his breastbone. "Got the wind knocked out of me, I guess."

"We need to clean that," Eli said, staring at Jimmy's leg.

Jimmy pinched his blood-smeared skin. He sucked his teeth as more red flowed from the wound.

"Don't touch it," Eli said, dropping his pack. "It'll get infected." He poured water from his canteen over the cuts. Jimmy winced as the blood flowed down his leg and soaked into his sock. Eli grabbed the first aid kit and tore open an antiseptic wipe. "This might sting a little," he said. He pressed the cloth into the cuts. Jimmy jerked his leg back and sucked in a quick breath. Eli tried to be as gentle as possible, but he needed to clean the wounds. "How far is the next town," Eli asked Will.

Will shook his head. "I don't think there is one before our next shelter. Why?"

Eli pulled the antiseptic wipe off Jimmy's leg. "We're almost out of these." He waved the wipe in the air. "It'll be all right, though." Eli squirted some antibacterial cream onto the cuts and bandaged them. Maggie stood over him, inches away, intently watching him work. A bubble swelled in Eli's chest. He felt self-conscious. He looked up at her. Despite the dirt and sweat, she was beautiful.

Dee pulled up in front of the sheriff's station. Ben's cruiser was parked outside. Her hands were shaking with anger and fear. She stepped out of her car and went inside.

The deputy sheriff jumped at the sound of the door opening. He was sitting behind the reception desk, surfing the internet.

Dee smiled tightly. "Hey, Daryl," she said. "I need to talk to Ben."

"Go right on back, Mrs. Sutton," he said. He looked like a child wearing his father's uniform.

Dee pushed the door to Ben's office open.

Ben was flipping through some paperwork. When he saw her, he stood. "Sit down, Dee," he said.

Dee remained standing. Ben did the same.

"Fifteen days, Ben."

Ben rubbed the back of his neck.

"Fifteen days. You told me more than a week ago that they set up a checkpoint on the Appalachian Trail and that Eli would be home safe and sound in no time."

"Dee, I—"

Dee held up her hand. "Fifteen days my boy's been out there, Ben. You say the police and rangers in three states have been notified. Well where is he, Ben? Why haven't they found him? Get out there and find him, Ben!"

Ben walked over to the office door and started to close it.

"You don't want your idiot deputy to hear?"

Ben gestured down the hallway to Daryl. "Come on, Dee."

That was uncalled for. He was right. She was just so angry. She was bubbling over. Her home was empty. At night, the walls creaked and the wind rattled her window. She never remembered hearing noises like that when Sam and Eli were around. She let her hand fall. Tears started pouring down her cheeks. "I'm sorry. I just ... I'm sorry."

Ben put his arms around her. "The search is on, Dee. I don't know why they didn't get him at the checkpoint. We talked about this, remember? They're looking for him all the way up through Virginia now."

Dee sobbed into Ben's uniform.

Jimmy was slowing them down. The cuts on his leg weren't too deep, but when he fell, his ankle had rolled. He stopped frequently to let it rest, and when they were hiking, he limped along.

The trail turned up, and the miles crept by as the afternoon grew long. Eli passed the time snatching glances of Maggie. He didn't notice the wall of solid gray advancing on them until trickles of rain began to fall and lightning sparked in the distance.

"I think we should hike off the trail and set up camp," Eli said as the gang stopped to don their rain gear.

"The next shelter is about four miles," Will said.

"Yeah, but with as slow as Jimmy is going, it's going to be nightfall before we make it there." Eli pointed to the clouds. "And that doesn't look good."

"I'm fine," Jimmy said. "I'll pick it up. We'll make it. It's just a few miles longer."

Eli shook his head. "Fine."

"Maybe Eli's right," Maggie said. "Maybe we'd be better off just setting up camp."

"It's only a bit farther," Will said.

Maggie looked at the clouds.

"Come on," Will said. "We'll make it." He slapped Jimmy on the back. "Stop being such a baby."

They started again. The rain speckled the trail, and the incline continued. Eli's legs pumped. He was in good shape; he could hike up hills for days. Maggie and Will also did well, but Jimmy continued to limp.

The rain fell harder and splattered their faces, dripping from their coats and down their legs. As they crested a bald ridge, the trees opened up and so did the sky. In all directions,

Eli could see valleys and hills coated in shadow. Blankets of rain poured across them. As the sun set, the valleys sank deeper into the shadows, disappearing in the mud and the rain.

Eli stopped and pulled on his headlamp. "This is stupid," he said. "We should have stopped and set up camp."

"Why don't we stop here, Will?" Maggie asked.

Will nodded his head. "Maybe we should. I'm getting soaked."

Eli shook his head. "And set up our tents on a high ridge in a storm? That's just brilliant. We'll get fried like chickens by morning."

"What?" Jimmy asked.

Right on cue, lightning flickered in the distance, followed a moment later by dull thunder.

"Oh," Jimmy said.

"We need to get off this ridge, and quick," Eli said.

They quickened the pace as much as Jimmy could handle, but the sky continued to flash. The clouds crackled with blues and purples, sparked with orange and white. The valley danced in the pulsating light. The shadows jumped in and out of existence and the thunder grew louder and closer to the flashes.

The trail turned rocky as the ridge peaked. Large boulders protruded from the path. Eli struggled to maintain his balance on the wet rock. Just ahead of him, Jimmy slipped and fell in the mud. Eli stopped to help him to his feet.

The rain drenched both of them in wet white noise. The pounding of the rain blotted out the sound of the wind and smeared the sound of their voices but seemed to make the thunder louder.

The lightning snapped overhead. In the flash Eli saw someone standing on the trail they'd just crossed. It was only the silhouette of a person, lit by the lightning and then eaten by the darkness. Eli pointed his headlamp toward the figure. He could see a dim shape, but the rain obscured all the details.

"You guys okay?" Maggie yelled. She was a few yards up the trail.

Eli turned. "I think there's someone back there." He spun around.

Boom!

White light blasted his eyes. For a second, the ridge was as bright as if the noon sun shined down on it. In the light he saw the figure on the trail. It was the same crazy man who had screamed in the berries, who had stared so strangely at Eli, and then, seemingly, disappeared. The light dispelled quickly, but as it did, Eli saw the man open his arms and lift off the ground.

"Holy crap!" Jimmy screamed, falling back into the mud.

Eli's ears rang. He wiggled his jaw as if he could dislodge the sound. "Did you see that?" Eli asked.

Jimmy wiped water from his face and rubbed his ears through the hood of his rain jacket. "Did I see the lightning that almost just killed us? Do you think I'm blind? I mean, I almost am now." Jimmy pressed on his eyes.

Eli looked back up the trail. His headlamp cut through the rain. Nothing was there. The scorched air smelled of burning metal. Eli's skin tingled with static. But he saw nothing on the trail.

"I think I saw ..." Eli meant to say "the Raven Mocker," but he couldn't get the words into his mouth. They clung to his lungs. He grabbed Jimmy by the hand and pulled him up. "Come on," he said. "We need to get out of here."

They trotted along as fast as they could, as fast as Jimmy could. The rain continued to pour. Eli looked over his shoulder every few steps, thinking that any minute the Raven Mocker might swoop down on them, grab him—or Maggie—and disappear again.

The lightning moved over the ridge and headed into the distance. With each flash, more time passed between the light and the thunder. The storm had crossed them. Soon, the lightning was only visible as bursts of purple and blue in the distant clouds, and the thunder lost its edge. The ridge sank and the water rushed down the trail. But Eli continued to look behind him. His headlamp lighted the fields and sky in a dim beam.

"What are you looking for?" Maggie asked.

Eli wasn't sure what to tell her. Would she believe him if he told her what he saw in the storm? He almost didn't believe himself. He blinked the rain from his eyes. "Just waiting for the storm to break."

After another mile or so, the trail led back into the woods. The white blazes, marked on rocks across the ridge, took to the trees again. Not long after that, Will shined his flashlight on a blue blaze. "Here's the trail to the shelter," he said.

They tromped down the path, boots squishing and lights searching for the blue rectangles. The trees crept in on them, and the shadows cast by their lamps and lights shot into the woods, where Eli imagined the Raven Mocker and U`tlun'ta sat watching them, the rain flooding the cracks and crevasses of the Raven Mocker's leathered skin and splattering off U`tlun'ta's rock-like flesh.

The sound of rain falling on tin reeled him in from his imagination. Eli shined his headlamp onto a stone shelter. They rushed inside, wet and frightened. Their lights filled the interior and cast overlapping shadows onto the walls and ceiling. The rain pounded on the roof.

Eli dropped his bag, wiped his face, and squeezed the water from his hair. Will should have listened to him. He ripped his pack open and pulled out a spare shirt. He threw his rain gear in the corner of the shelter and wiped his face.

"Got something to say?" Will asked.

Eli stopped drying his hair. He did have something to say. They could have been killed up there. Eli turned to Will. Eli was a full foot shorter than him. If they were to get in a fight, he'd get pummeled. He kept his voice calm despite the anger swelling in his chest. "We could have died on that ridge. We should have stopped and set up tents when it started raining.

I'm hiking alone tomorrow." Eli shook his head. "I'll leave before breakfast and get ahead of you."

"We don't need you," Will said. "So go."

Jimmy and Maggie both looked from Eli to Will and back again.

"I'd like it if you didn't leave," Maggie said.

Jimmy nodded his head. "Me too."

Will seemed about ready to say something, but then his jaw clenched tight and he turned away. He tore into his pack and jerked his sleeping bag out. He unrolled it and tossed it on the wood in a puff of anger and dust.

Jimmy and Maggie both took off their rain gear. Maggie began drying her hair. Eli watched her as he pulled his sleeping bag from his pack and laid down on it.

After a moment of silence, Jimmy said, "Is no one hungry?"

Maggie laughed. The sound filled the shelter. It drowned out Eli's anger and the sound of the rain. Eli was hungry. He rolled over on his side. "Anyone want to go collect wood?"

Maggie and Jimmy scrunched their faces as the sound of rain on tin continued. Will stared at the ceiling, motionless, silent.

"Granola bars it is," Eli said. He propped himself against the shelter wall. The stone was cold.

Maggie sat next to him. "I think that's all we have anyhow."

Jimmy laughed and looked at Will. "How far is the next town?" No reply. "Will?"

"Look it up yourself, Jimmy. You don't know how a book works?" Will turned his back to the group.

Another moment of silence spread into the shelter, and the strumming rain slowed. "Where is it?" Jimmy asked.

Will picked his pack up and threw it at Jimmy. Then he rolled back on his side, facing the wall.

Jimmy frowned at Maggie. Her eyes were wide, but she said nothing. She only shrugged her shoulders. Jimmy dug into Will's pack, looking for the guidebook.

Eli tore open a granola bar and handed the box to Maggie. As she opened one, Eli pulled out his grandfather's journal, unzipped the plastic bag, and slipped it from his father's silk handkerchief.

Maggie tapped the journal. "You're always reading that. What is it?"

"It's my grandad's journal."

Maggie took a bite of the granola bar. She rubbed the silk handkerchief between her fingers. "You mind if I read a little with you?"

Eli shook his head. Maggie scooted closer to him. Their shoulders touched, and the granola stuck in Eli's throat.

April 2nd, 1935

I left today. I walked along a road that led into the woods. I didn't know where I was going. I just left. I just couldn't stay in that house any longer, the house where Mother died, the house where my dad is frozen, forever staring out the window.

I walked down the road for several miles and then I saw a path in the woods. I followed it. I walked all day. I'm out here in the woods now, alone, and I can finally feel the time passing again. I miss Mother terribly, and I should be there for Dad, but right now, I can't stand the thought of going back. In the morning, I'm going to keep following this path and see where it takes me.

Within minutes, Maggie was asleep on Eli's shoulder. He didn't move. He wanted that moment—that closeness—to last forever.

He read the journal entry again. It was the entry that inspired him to leave his home. He read the last line, let it fill his mouth. It was good advice. More people should just follow the path in front of them, Eli supposed, and see where it takes them. He closed the journal, wrapped it back in the silk handkerchief, and sealed it in the bag.

The next morning, Will didn't say much, and Jimmy, Maggie, and Eli ignored the argument from the night before. Eli had planned to leave the group, but after the previous night, after Maggie had fallen asleep next to him—well, he needed to refill his food supply just as much as they did. No sense in breaking off from the group before that was done. He would follow the path and see where it took him.

They left the AT and hiked to a narrow paved road that led into a small town called Sugar Grove. Jimmy limped the whole way. It was mid-morning and hot already, but the discomfort was mostly caused by the rain from the day before as humidity filled the air. Sweat dripped down Eli's face and soaked his chest, armpits, and pack straps.

Will stuck his thumb out as cars passed them. A pickup stopped after a few minutes. A woman smiled at them from the driver's seat. "Y'all AT hikers?" she said.

They all nodded.

"Going into Sugar Grove for groceries?"

They nodded more. The heat was too much. Even talking was a chore. Eli wanted to be back in the woods, where the canopy kept him cool.

"Well, get in," the woman said.

Will reached for the passenger door.

"Honey, no offense," the woman said, "but I can smell you from here. I'd prefer you rode in the bed."

They threw their packs in the pickup and hopped in. Eli helped Jimmy over the tailgate. Jimmy laughed as the truck pulled back onto the road. "Yeah, you smell like crap, Will."

"Shut up, Jimmy," Will said.

"I'm just joking," Jimmy said. "Don't be so sensitive."

Will said nothing more.

They were flying down the road. It was an odd sensation, such fast movement and feeling the rush of air after days spent walking. Eli stuck his hand into the wind and it pressed against his skin. He flexed his arm against the pressure, and he cupped the air in his palm, wrapped his fingers around it, held an invisible object. Eli had walked through that air every day, that thin fog that covered the planet, and never really noticed it, never really felt it until then. The wind tousled his hair, rippled his skin. Pushing and rushing, that wind was unfamiliar to him. All in the palm of his hand, right against the skin, right against that thin layer of himself, the last intimate protective layer of self he had.

Dark lines crisscrossed over his vision, the flutter of his lashes blowing in the wind. In the distance, the land was still. The sky, perfect blue above, faded to violet, to rose, to dark-green mountains, mountains that would have been tall if it weren't for the sky pressing down on them, dwarfing them in its immensity.

Eli absently touched the knife in his pocket. He imagined his grandfather walking along that road, or a road like it. He tried to picture the landscape then. The forest was probably very similar, but other things had changed. Telephone poles lined the road, thick cables stretching between them. Back then, none of those would have been there. There was no electricity in that part of the country then. Eli imagined the homes they passed were different as well. Most of the buildings he saw were brick and the sheds were all aluminum. Eli's grandfather had probably seen mostly wooden structures, as wood was readily available in the surrounding forest.

The pickup rolled on, its steady rumbling filling the space around them with noise and the smell of oil. It smelled like his father, who always wore a hint of gas and a dash of the earth's scent. Eli wiped a tear from his eye before Maggie saw it.

The pickup slowed and pulled into a parking lot. Eli, Maggie, and Will hopped out. Jimmy slowly lowered himself to the ground. Eli thanked the woman and set his pack down outside of a small food mart. Jimmy leaned against the building's brick wall.

"I don't know about this," he said, and unlaced his boot.

"What do you mean?" Will asked.

Jimmy squinted up at him. "I don't think I'm going to keep going. My ankle is killing me, and after——" Jimmy stopped himself.

"After what?" Will said.

Jimmy looked at his boots. "After yesterday. After you——"

Will scoffed and went inside.

Maggie bent down next to Jimmy. "If your ankle hurts, I think you should stay off it for a while. What if we set up camp here for a few days and let you rest?"

Jimmy shook his head. "Nah, I think I'm just going to call my mom. I checked the map last night. We're not that far from home. I think my mom could be up here in a few hours."

"Well, whatever you think is best, Jimmy," Maggie said.

"Does Will have his phone on him?" Jimmy asked.

"I think so," Maggie said. "I'll go ask."

Eli stopped her. "You can use my phone." Eli had no problem with Jimmy calling it quits. He liked him, but with him off the trail, they could pick up the pace again.

Eli dug his phone from his pack and opened the bag it was in. He turned it on and handed it to Jimmy.

After a moment, Jimmy said, "You have a ton of messages. This thing is blowing up with alerts."

Eli grabbed the phone from him. His mom had probably tried calling him a million times. "What's the number? I'll just dial it for you," he said.

Maggie eyed him. Eli could feel her curiosity heighten as he punched the numbers and handed the phone to Jimmy.

Will stuck his head out the door. "You guys getting food or what?"

"Jimmy's calling his mom," Maggie said. "His ankle is hurting him too bad to keep going."

Will rolled his eyes and went back inside.

"You want me to get you anything to eat?" Maggie asked Jimmy.

Jimmy turned the phone away from his mouth. "Jerky," he said, "and ice cream. And something to drink." He pressed the phone to his ear. "Mom?"

Maggie and Eli left him to his call. The store was air conditioned. Cool air had never felt so good in all of Eli's life. A girl sat behind the counter. She hardly looked older than Maggie. Eli walked by her and into the dairy aisle. He opened a freezer and felt the cold rush around him. He tossed a few ice cream sandwiches in his basket and continued shopping. He grabbed the usual: pasta, dried fruit, trail mix, granola bars. After more than two weeks, he was getting a little tired of the same stuff, but dry food was the easiest, and if he meant to make it to Maine, he needed to keep his pack light and his head clear.

He also picked up some moleskin and antiseptic wipes to replenish his supply. He passed a sign for the restrooms and stopped. He held his basket out to Maggie. "Can you watch this for a second? I just need to use the bathroom."

Maggie took his basket in her free hand and wandered down another aisle. Eli watched her for a moment and then turned up a narrow hallway toward the restroom. The door was locked. Eli stood in the hallway, which was filled with boxes of soda and chips. A corkboard hung on one wall. A few flyers plastered its surface, along with some work safety posters. Eli's jaw dropped, though, when he saw a flyer with his face on it. He ripped it down as the bathroom lock snapped open behind him. He spun, hiding the flyer behind his back.

Will walked out of the bathroom. Had he seen the flyer with Eli's face on it before going into the restroom? Eli had no idea.

Eli closed the bathroom door and leaned against it. He held up the flyer. "Missing" was at the top in bold letters. Beneath that was a description of him, his name, hometown, and the photo, along with several numbers to call if anyone saw him, including his mother's. Eli folded the paper and stuck it in his pocket. Had the girl at the counter recognized him? He didn't think so. He would just buy the groceries and they would get back on the trail. He washed his hands and face and looked in the mirror. Pretty pink scars. He shook his head and opened the door.

He walked back up the narrow hall and paused. He eyed the clerk. She was reading a magazine. He kept his head turned away from her as he walked down the aisle where Maggie was. "Thanks," he said to Maggie as he took his basket from her. He snuck another glance at the clerk. She twirled her hair and flipped a page of the magazine.

Eli grabbed a few more items and then swallowed. He was tempted to give Maggie some money and let her buy his groceries, but what would he tell Maggie the reason was? He bit his lip and took a breath. He approached the counter, trying to keep his head turned away. He looked at a rack of gum as he set his basket on the counter.

The clerk closed her magazine and started taking the food out of Eli's basket. Maggie grabbed another box of granola bars and stepped in line behind him. Eli kept his face turned away from the clerk. Maggie smiled at him.

"Hikers?" the girl asked.

Eli nodded. Maggie raised her eyebrows at him. Suddenly it was awkward that he wasn't looking at the clerk. He turned back to the counter, hoping that she wouldn't recognize him.

"Sure are," Maggie said.

Eli felt a waterfall of sweat on his forehead.

"Where y'all comin' from?"

Eli's throat closed. He didn't want to say Tennessee. In a squeak, he said, "Georgia."

"Georgia?" Maggie burst out. "I thought you said you were from Tennessee?"

Eli stammered. The words were there, they just couldn't quite stand on his tongue. After what seemed like an eternity, he said, "That's what I meant. Tennessee. What was I thinking?" He swallowed hard.

"Don't know," the clerk said. "Thirty-one, seventy-six."

Eli handed her cash and grabbed the bags from the counter. The heat blasted him as he left the store. He dropped the bags on the sidewalk and started stuffing the food into his pack, throwing away the unnecessary packaging.

Maggie came out a moment later, followed by Will. "Georgia. You're crazy," she said. "You forgot where you were from?" She set down her bags and smiled at Eli. "You got a crush on that girl?"

Eli blushed. "No, I just—" He didn't have an excuse. "It's just the heat, I guess."

"It is hot," Maggie said. "I don't remember it ever getting this hot where I'm from. I guess that can't be right, though. Right? I mean, the weather can't change that much in just a few hours' drive, can it? I don't know."

Maggie could talk to herself for hours. It was cute.

They loaded their packs. Jimmy watched them. His mom was coming to pick him up in a few hours. Will, Maggie, and Eli drank some water and refilled their canteens at a spigot on the side of the building. Then they stood next to their packs in front of Jimmy.

"I can't believe you're quitting," Will said, shaking his head.

"I can hardly walk. My ankle's all swollen. I'd just be a burden from here on." Jimmy squinted at the road behind them. "And really? I'm kind of tired of hiking." He laughed. "I thought it would be more fun, but every day is the same thing."

"Whatever," Will said. "I'll see you when I get back."
Will and Jimmy shook hands.

"Aw, are you guys friends again?" Maggie said
half-genuinely and half-sarcastically.

"Shut up, Maggie." Will didn't look at her. He just picked
up his pack and started walking toward the road.

Eli almost said something to him, but then Jimmy slapped
him on the back. "Take it easy, Tenneblind," he said. "If that
is your real name." Jimmy laughed.

Eli shook his hand. "Good luck." He hoisted his pack onto
his back and lingered as Maggie and Jimmy said goodbye.
Then Maggie hugged Jimmy. Jimmy wrapped his thin arms
around her. Eli raised his eyes to the sky. He pretended he
didn't care, pretended he didn't see Jimmy's hands touch
Maggie's hair, pretended he didn't see Maggie's bare knees
touch Jimmy's skinny legs. Then the hug was over and
Maggie scooped up her pack.

Eli and Maggie rushed to catch up with Will, leaving
Jimmy at the store with an ice cream sandwich, a bag of
jerky, and a soda.

They hiked all afternoon and stopped at the first shelter
they came to. It was a big log cabin and had two other people
occupying it when they arrived. A man and woman sat at the
picnic table outside. Eli slowed as he walked toward them,
but Maggie and Will quickened their pace.

"Do you mind if we join you for the night?" Maggie asked.
"This place sure looks big enough."

"No problem," the man said. He put down the book he was reading. "My name's Groundhog and this is my wife, Stilts."

"Groundhog and Stilts?" Maggie said. "I like that. Good names." She introduced Will, Eli, and herself using their trail names. "I got to say," she continued, "you two look like you've only been on the trail an hour compared to us."

Stilts laughed. "This shelter is better than most hotels. There's a shower around the corner, just there."

Maggie's jaw dropped. "A shower! Oh my goodness. I call it first."

While Maggie showered, Eli pulled his freshest clothes from his pack and set them aside. There also was a water spigot at the shelter. They wouldn't need to boil water. And he could rinse the sweat from the clothes he had on, wring them out, and let them dry overnight. He was beginning to feel pretty gross. This was just what he needed.

Maggie came out of the shower. Her hair was wet and clean and beautiful. Eli stared at her, maybe just a second too long. He glanced at his feet and then up at Will.

"You want to go next?" Eli said.

"Whatever," Will said. "Go ahead." Will didn't look at him.

Eli took his cleaner clothes to the shower and stripped down. The water felt great. It was the first warm shower he'd had in more than two weeks. Until then, he had only cleaned himself in rivers and rain. When he returned home, he would never go a day without showering again.

He collected his clothes and walked out of the shower room feeling a million times better. The cleansing power of water went beyond the skin.

Eli put his clothes next to his pack. He planned to wash them and hang them to dry. First, though, he just wanted to relax a little. He sat down next to Maggie, who was cooking some pasta over the fire.

Will silently headed for the shower. Suddenly, something felt wrong to Eli. It clicked almost immediately. He moved as quickly as he could over to his dirty clothes. His heart rushed as he dug through the pockets of his dirty shorts. The poster with his face on it was gone. It must have slipped from his pocket. He pushed into the shower room.

"What the hell?" Will said, looking up.

The poster was still folded and on the ground. Eli grabbed it and turned for the door. "Sorry," he said. "I just dropped something."

Eli put the poster in his pack and flipped it closed. He should have thrown it away in the bathroom at the food mart.

The following day was Father's Day. Will turned on his phone and searched for reception so that he and Maggie could call their fathers. He wandered back and forth on the trail, holding his phone in front of him.

Eli sat on a stump and waited. In front of him, grass rolled in the breeze, and wildflowers soaked up the sun. Beyond that, hills spread to the horizon.

Maggie sat next to him. "You going to call your dad? I bet he'd like to talk to you. I know mine would. He's probably just sitting on the back porch right now, drinking some iced tea. It's hot today. I bet—"

"He's dead," Eli said.

Maggie turned to him. The space between them filled with awkward silence. "What?" Maggie asked.

"My dad. He's dead. He died in a car accident. The one I got these scars in." Eli pointed to his face.

"I'm so sorry." Maggie looked at her boots, her boots that had walked almost as much as she'd talked. They were both quiet and still. "I didn't know."

The pasture blurred. Eli blinked his tears away, not wanting Maggie to see, but more came, a rush of them that obscured the shape of the land. They weren't hills and valleys any longer. They were light and dark with shades of green in between. The divisions grew larger as more water flooded his eyes.

"I'm sorry, Eli," Maggie said. She touched his hand.

Eli stared into the blurry field. His heart pounded. He missed his father so much. He missed his mom, too. And yet there he was, sitting on a stump in Virginia, and all he wanted was to reach out and hug the girl next to him. If he could just embrace her, everything would be better. Then the blur of green suddenly was streaked with brown. Several horses walked on to the field from the forest, their hair almost orange, their heads low to the ground, mouths nibbling at the grass.

Eli wiped the tears away. A few of the horses were pinto, dappled white like someone had dropped buckets of paint on them. Eli pointed at them, thankful when Maggie looked away.

"Oh my goodness," Maggie said. "They're beautiful. Whose do you think they are?"

A few of the horses perked up, raised their heads, their ears turning to catch the sound of Maggie's voice. A young colt trotted and played next to his mother. His legs were long and thin and wobbly, but they would grow strong someday.

"I don't think they belong to anyone," Eli said, glad the conversation was changing course. He dried his eyes.

Maggie smiled at him. "You think they're wild? That's crazy. There're just wild horses up here? Why doesn't someone gather them up? Sell them?"

Eli settled on the only answer that made sense. "Because they don't belong to anyone."

"I know," Maggie said, "but they could. Someone could claim them."

Eli suddenly felt something arise inside him; it was like someone had been gathering stones for months and stacking them to build a wall, but the stones had kept falling over, slipping off each other. But the wall was taking form, held together by Eli's anger. "You're right," he said, hearing his voice but feeling someone else's words on his tongue. "We've claimed everything else." He waved his hand toward the trees. "Not even the forest belongs to itself anymore. Why not just box and pen everything? Cram all the squirrels and birds into cages and hang them from the branches of the trees so they can't roam the forest." Eli had never spoken so quickly in his life, never fit his thoughts into words so perfectly. "Take all this and shove it in a dusty corral." He held his hands out to the horses as if he could scoop them up into his palm. "Break it and tame it before it does the opposite to you—before it makes you wild." Eli looked at Maggie. "Isn't that what bothers you?" he said.

"I'm not sure what you're asking," Maggie said, looking from the horses to Eli.

"It bothers you that these horses aren't owned by anyone."

"Well, it doesn't bother me. I just thought it was strange that they aren't. I've never seen a wild horse."

"And that doesn't seem strange to you? The fact that you think all the horses in the world should be owned by people? That doesn't seem odd?"

"I guess. I don't know." Maggie smiled at Eli. She looked really pretty. "You're talkative today. Usually you're so quiet." A tiny bit of silence connected them. Then Maggie said, "I'm sorry again about your dad. I didn't know."

Eli nodded. He felt the stone wall inside him crumble. "It's okay." His fingers slipped into his pocket and removed the knife. "This was his. He used it to carve his name in a tree on Mount Katahdin. My grandfather did too." Eli rubbed the handle with his thumb. "That's where I'm going." He said the last part to the field.

Maggie's fingers lightly touched his as she reached for the knife. "Can I look?"

Eli let her take the knife from him.

"It's old. Maybe older than your pack." She pushed his shoulder playfully.

Eli let himself smile.

"You've got a great smile. You should wear it more often," Maggie said, staring at his lips. Again, silence hovered between them, drawing them closer. Maggie touched Eli's leg and leaned toward him.

Their lips touched: soft, wet.

Will pushed through the brush to Eli's right. Maggie pulled back, her cheeks glowing red.

"I can't get any stinkin' bars," Will said, staring at his phone. "We can try again later."

Eli looked at Maggie, but she avoided his eyes.

A few miles later, they hiked out of the gap they were in. Will took his phone out and had full service. While Will and Maggie called their fathers, Eli fired stones into the forest with his wrist rocket. Oddly shaped stones, or stones that were too large, flew slow and tended to curve off target. But a round stone, a smooth stone, would buzz through the air, straight as an arrow. Eli had learned from experience. He gathered several dozen good stones and pocketed them. He fired a few, hitting branches and leaves with ease.

The trail led them to Chatfield Memorial Shelter. In front of the shelter there were short stone walls covered in green moss.

"I'm so thirsty," Will said, dropping his pack. He gulped water from his canteen. "I'll get water if you start a fire."

Maggie and Eli began gathering twigs as Will left. Eli started to say something about their kiss, but when he opened his mouth all that came out was, "Will's in a better mood." What was that? What was he talking about Will for?

Maggie laughed. "Talking to his dad always straightens him out."

Eli nodded, swallowed, and opened his mouth again. Words closer to what he actually wanted to say came out. "I really like you, Maggie. I—"

She leaned over and kissed him. Then she pulled away. "Don't tell Will."

Eli was out of breath, his words gone again.

Will returned with a pot of water. He set it and his canteen on the table.

Maggie tossed her collected kindling by the fire pit and turned her canteen up, shaking out the last drops. "Can I get a drink out of yours?" she asked Will.

"Sure," Will said.

She took the canteen from him. Wiping the water from her mouth, she offered it to Eli. "You out too?"

Eli nodded and took the canteen. The water filled his mouth.

The days grew longer. Each one seemed to drag through the woods as roughly as the trail did, over stones and roots, gullies and rivers. There was lots of silence on the trail. Maggie sometimes whistled and chatted about the trees and the birds, but she mostly stayed quiet while they hiked, reserving her lungs for breathing. Will and Eli did the same. The sound of their boots on the dirt and rocks filled the space. Sometimes the leaves tickled the wind and birds called to each other, seemed to follow them even. But when the trail turned up, the sound of lost breath and nothing else rang in Eli's ears.

Mostly, the days passed in silence until night, when they would shake the dusty packs from their shoulders and sit around the fire. Some nights, if Will went to fetch water or to the bathroom, leaving Eli and Maggie momentarily alone, Maggie would reach for Eli. Their lips would briefly touch, their skin tingling as their fingers mingled. Other nights, when Will never left camp, Eli would pull out his grandfather's journal and set the silk handkerchief next to Maggie. While he reread the journal, she would rub the silk between her fingers.

Mid-June, I suspect

I lost track of the days. I've been out here for weeks now, living on the trail, living on the land. The Appalachian Mountains are unforgiving, but it feels good to walk. Every day that passes, every mile that passes, I feel better. I miss Mother. I think I will as long as I'm alive. The pain surges up periodically, from somewhere deep inside me, like a geyser blowing steam into the air. Then, it settles back down and is nothing more than a hole in the ground.

I'm not sure how far I've come or how much farther I'll go. The path will lead me as far as I need, I suppose. I trust the earth to tell me when I should return home. I hope Dad's not worried about me. I wonder where Robert is. Surely he's gotten word of Mother's death by now. I wonder if he's on his way to Grandad's new farm.

Late June or early July

The woods are a strange place. After a while spent in them, you get the feeling that the trees know you're here. Perhaps that's where the stories of the Yunwi Tsunsdi come from. They are a presence among the forest, an intelligent and caring presence.

Fear is also out here. It creeps through the trees like wisps of smoke, here one moment and gone the next. Are U' tlun'ta and the Raven Mocker out there? I think I see them sometimes, walking through the trees or disguised as animals, crawling among the muck. They can't be real, though. It's just my fear taking form.

When I see them, though, I miss Coal Creek. I miss the north field, the rows of corn. I miss life there more than I miss Knoxville. We had a community. I didn't realize how important that was until now, until I spent time alone.

Eli woke up in the middle of the night. His sleeping bag was soaked in sweat. He was lying on his side, holding his stomach. It cramped every few seconds. He reached for his flashlight. He felt like he was turning inside out, his stomach clawing its way up his throat. He threw his sleeping bag open and ran into the woods.

He vomited. When he was finished, he returned to the shelter. His head glided among the stars as he walked, like his brain was inside a helium balloon tied around his neck. His skin sticky with sweat, he fell asleep.

He woke up a few hours later to the sound of his watch's alarm. He crawled from the sleeping bag and sat on the edge of the shelter.

Maggie walked around the corner. Her face was pale and her hair clung in wet strands to her skin. "You don't look so good," she said to Eli.

He started to force a laugh but was too nauseous to finish. "You don't look so good either. Feeling okay?"

"I've been sick all morning."

Eli turned. Behind him, the shelter was empty. "Where's Will?"

Maggie sat down next to Eli and pointed into the woods.

"Vomiting?" Eli asked.

"Or diarrhea. I didn't ask." Maggie rested her head on Eli's shoulder.

Eli reached up and touched her cheek.

They got a slow start that morning. All three of their bellies were rumbling, and they all groaned about their heads spinning. Their pace was slower and they had to take many breaks, but they did hike. The day was long, the sultry air heavy and hard to walk through. The mosquitoes seemed more prevalent, biting at their exposed skin, causing them to slap their necks and knees. The climbs seemed more arduous, with more rocks in their path and steeper inclines.

They stopped for almost an hour at lunch, though no one ate much. Eli nibbled at a granola bar half-heartedly. Maggie and Will both rested their heads on their packs and closed their eyes. Eli flipped to the last passage in his grandfather's journal and read it over and over again.

Late July, perhaps

I'm at my trail's end. The earth is different up here. From the flat rock ledge where I'm sitting looking out across the landscape, the world is beautiful. To the west, a large valley and mountain. To the north, cliffs. To the east, rolling blue ridges surrounding several valleys filled with thick forest and lush grass, filled with life.

I feel my life will never be the same after this, but it's time I returned home. I carved my name in a tree just south of the ledge. Maybe one day I'll come back here and see how I've grown.

Eli had a long way to go before he would be at his trail's end. He rubbed the knife in his pocket.

They hiked the rest of the afternoon. As soon as they made it to the shelter, Eli ripped open his pack and grabbed a roll of toilet paper and his shovel. His pack fell over as he ran into the woods. His clothes and food and things spilled onto the ground.

He squatted in the woods. A gnat buzzed in his ear, and he swatted it away. When he was done, he stood up. His head spun, but he felt slightly better. He headed back to the shelter.

When he returned, Will was holding the flyer from the grocery store.

"What the hell, man?" Will said. "You're some sort of fugitive? A runaway?"

"Why are you rummaging through my stuff?" Eli tried to snatch the poster from Will, but his muscles were moving too slowly and his vision was off.

"I can't believe this. We've been hiking for two weeks with you," Will said. He turned to Maggie. "We have to call the Forest Service."

"I'm confused," Maggie said, looking at the flyer. "You told me your name was Eli Jack. Why'd you run away? I don't understand."

"It doesn't matter; it's definitely him. He's Eli Sutton. Look at the picture," Will said. "Your mom's number is on here. I'm going to call her." He reached into his pack and grabbed his phone.

Eli didn't know what to do. His first instinct was to run, just run into the woods. But his legs were shaky and his stomach worse. Also, he couldn't just leave Maggie. "Don't. Please don't," he said. He sat down and put his head in his hands. "I need to make it to Mount Katahdin. For my father and grandfather."

"What are you talking about?" Will said.

Maggie turned to Will. "His dad—"

Will cut her off. "How long have you been out here?" he asked Eli.

"A few weeks," Eli said.

Maggie clenched her stomach and ran toward the woods, but she only made it a few feet. She vomited.

"Oh my God," Will said. "Are you okay?" He set the phone and the flyer down and reached out to hold Maggie's hair.

"I don't understand," Eli said. "We haven't eaten any spoiled food and we've boiled all our water." Eli looked at Maggie. She was wiping her mouth. He wanted to hug her, say it would be all right, to hold her.

Will looked at his canteen. His shoulders drooped and his eyes widened. "I haven't," he said quietly.

Eli turned to him. "You haven't what?"

"A few days ago," Will said, "I filled my canteen from the river."

Eli shook his head. "Why would we all be sick?" he said. "I've only filled my canteen with water I knew was boiled."

"It was several days ago. I didn't think about it. The water was crystal clear. When I came back to the shelter, Maggie asked me for a drink, and she also handed the canteen to you."

Maggie stood. Her skin was tinted green.

Eli remembered. It was the day they saw the horses. The day he and Maggie first kissed. "You idiot," he whispered. Then his voice grew stronger. "Do you know what kind of diseases you can get from untreated water? Who knows what we got."

"Hey, I'm not the idiot." Will looked at Maggie. "If it wasn't for him, Jimmy wouldn't have gotten hurt and had to quit," he said.

"What are you talking about?" Maggie said. "What does that have to do with you filling your canteen from the river?"

"I'm just saying," Will said.

"Even so, how do you figure that's Eli's fault? Jimmy tripped," Maggie said.

"You guys wouldn't have been in the field if he didn't lead you down there."

"Jimmy was the first one through the fence. You're crazy, Will. This is all crazy. You're the one that's supposed to be leading this trip, and you're acting like a jerk. You have been since we started."

"I'm acting like a jerk?" Will said. "This is the guy who ran away from home." He reached for the flyer, but Eli grabbed it first. "Give it to me," Will demanded.

Eli shook his head.

Will picked up his phone. "I'll just call the Forest Service, then. They'll come pick you up and take you home to your mommy."

"Don't," Eli said.

"What are you going to do about it?" Will said. He lunged for the paper in Eli's hand but missed.

Eli stood, stepping away from Will. Will tried to snatch the paper again, but Eli pulled it out of reach. Will eyed him and then shoved him. Eli tripped over a rock and tumbled to the ground. Will leaned down and tried to grab the paper from Eli, but Eli crumpled it into his fist. Will punched him in the arm. His fist was the size of sledgehammer.

"Give it to me," Will said. He continued hitting Eli in the arm.

Eli turned on his side, grabbed Will's ankle, and pulled. Will shifted his weight and fell to the ground. He clenched his jaw and scrambled on top of Eli, pressing Eli's breath out of him, and ripped the paper from his hand. Eli squirmed underneath him and tried to grab it back, but Will held it in the air as he sat on Eli's stomach and pushed his face into the dirt.

"Stop it, Will!" Maggie yelled.

Eli bucked and tried to scramble from under him, but Will hardly moved. Eli could feel his face turn red, could feel Maggie's eyes on him. He curled his fist and threw a punch. It connected weakly with Will's shoulder.

"You want to take it to the next level?" Will said. He let go of Eli's face, drew his fist back, and let it fly.

Eli's jaw exploded in pain. He'd never been in a fight before. He threw his arms up as Will punched him in the side of the head. Eli's skull slammed into the ground.

"Quit it!" Maggie screamed.

Eli stopped struggling. He just held his arms over his head for protection.

Will slowly stood up, lifting himself from the ground in a series of steps. Eli stayed on the ground.

"Why are you such a jerk?" Maggie said. She shoved Will with both hands, though hardly moved him.

Will brushed her off and wiggled the paper in the air. "I'm calling his mom. She needs to know he's out here." He turned on his phone.

Maggie leaned down next to Eli. "Are you okay?" She touched his head.

"There's no reception," Will said. He held his phone in the air, searching for a signal.

Maggie helped Eli up.

"That's it then," Eli said. "I'm going to fail my father. I'm going to take my blindfold off before morning."

"Blindfold?" Maggie asked.

Eli shook his head. "Nothing."

"What the hell's he talking about?" Will asked.

Maggie looked at Will with disgust. "His dad died not long ago."

Will shook his head and let his arms fall to his sides. "And you ran away? Left your mom?" Will asked. "That's awful, man. How could—"

Maggie spun and slapped Will.

Will's face turned red. He waved the flyer and his phone in Maggie's face. "Tomorrow morning. I'm calling his mom tomorrow morning. And if I can't get any bars, I'm stopping at the first town we come to and turning him in." Will stomped into the forest.

"I'm sorry," Maggie said.

Eli kicked the dirt. "I'm leaving."

"It's almost dark."

"In the morning then." Eli looked into the forest. Where were the Yunwi Tsunsdi when he needed them? "I'll wake up a few hours early."

"Will's still going to call your mom."

"It doesn't matter. I'll get ahead of you two and I'll stay off the trail where I can." Eli turned to Maggie. "I have to reach Mount Katahdin." He felt the pocketknife. "I have to carve my name below my father's. I don't want to stop hiking with you, but I don't have a choice."

Maggie pushed her hair back. "I'll come with you then."

That night, there was no fire. Maggie didn't sing and Eli didn't read his grandfather's journal. The crickets played their instruments though, and Eli stared into the darkness.

Eli and Maggie slipped away, leaving Will snoring in the shelter. Eli's stomach flipped and flopped as they hiked, and Maggie walked into the woods twice to vomit. Eli didn't feel much better. His feet were dragging on the trail. His boots felt heavy. Gummy sweat plastered his skin. But he hiked on anyway, and Maggie followed.

As the sun began to rise, they stopped to eat breakfast. Eli opened a granola bar. Its gritty surface was pocked with raisins. He wrapped it back up and stuck it in his pack. He drank some water instead as Maggie picked at a handful of trail mix.

They started again and hiked in silence. Nausea followed them, leaping out here and there and punching them in the stomachs. Randomly, one or the other would walk into the woods, saying nothing. The one left on the trail would take the time to rest until the other returned. Then they would hike on. Snails may have made more progress.

Mid-morning, Maggie stopped to rest. She looked at Eli. "I'm willing to bet that Will has called your mom by now and probably the forest rangers too."

The forest swam around Eli. He felt lightheaded. He didn't know what he was going to do. "I'm not stopping," he said, "if that's what you're suggesting."

"I'm not suggesting that." Maggie looked into the forest. She looked tired. "But if there's a ranger station anywhere on the trail in front of us, they'll stop us."

Eli looked at the trees. "Then we won't follow the trail." He picked up his bag and walked into the woods.

Maggie hesitated a moment. She looked up and down the trail, then followed Eli.

Dee sat on the couch. The television was muted. She watched the images on the screen: flickering, meaningless, but somehow comforting all the same. The phone rang.

She leaned over and picked it up. It was a number she didn't recognize. "Hello?"

"Is this Mrs. Sutton?" a young man's voice asked her.

"Yes it is."

"Mrs. Sutton, my name's Will and I've been hiking on the Appalachian Trail with your son, Eli, for the last couple of weeks."

"Oh my God." Dee couldn't believe it. "Is he okay? Let me talk to him."

"He's fine, but he's no longer with me. He ran off this morning with my sister."

Dee was confused. "What? How did you get my number? Where did he go? Where are you?" Too many questions on the tongue, all demanding space.

Will told her about meeting Eli, about hiking with him, about finding the flyer. When he was finished, Dee took his number down and told him to stay where he was. She called Ben.

The forest where they walked was thick and hard to navigate. Fallen trees and rocks stood in their way, and vines tripped them. Ferns, so prehistoric in appearance, held their fronds open to the sky, catching the sun that trickled from the canopy. Pea-sized purple flowers peppered thorn-strewn bushes that scratched their legs and snagged their clothes. The forest fought them at every step, tried to swallow them.

They pushed through the forest for a few hours. Each mile passed slowly, cruelly. Maggie vomited once more, nothing but dry heaves. It sounded out of place among the bird calls. There was nothing in her stomach anymore, not even water.

Eli checked his map and used his compass to keep them going in the same direction as the trail. It was hard to focus. His stomach cramped and he had to stop once an hour or more, silently walking away from Maggie into the woods to do his business. The little food that he had left didn't interest him. But he walked on, looking behind him every few yards to ensure Maggie was okay. Her eyes were glossy and her pace was slow, but she still walked.

Eli hoped the sickness was only temporary. If they hiked nice and slow, perhaps they would feel better in a day or two and could pick up their pace again. If they stayed off the trail, especially while they were moving slowly, they should be fine. As long as they walked in straight lines, they would reach sections of the AT and could reorient themselves. The more time they spent off the trail, the better.

Eli squatted in the woods. Not only was he running low on food, he was almost out of toilet paper. He stared into the thick. His eyes unfocused. The green blurred together. A smear of leaves, of shadow and light. Then a face jumped out at him.

U`tlun'ta glared at him from the leaves. Her eyes were black dots sunken in sockets of stone. He pinched his eyes closed and popped them open wide, focusing his vision as his heart flipped. The green blur took shape again as a forest. He saw that it wasn't U`tlun'ta at all. It was only the surface of a wall of rocks hidden by leaves. Vines poured over the rocks like a waterfall and clovers pooled at its base, covering the wet soil. Water spiders skated on puddles in the mud. The forest seemed to flow, gently drifting, almost imperceptibly so. The forest wasn't stationary. It just didn't go anywhere fast. Over time, it shifted as much as any sea, changed as much as any city.

Eli stood. He felt cold, though his skin was hot. As he walked back to where he'd left Maggie, he rubbed the pocketknife. Images of his father flipped through his mind from the car crash backward. Time flipped backward. Eli saw his grandfather and father, both still alive. His father was in the driveway tinkering with their car. His grandfather sat on their porch sipping a glass of iced tea.

"Careful over there, Eli," his father called.

Eli turned and saw himself. He was playing in the grass just beyond the porch. He was very young.

"Don't go near that old well," his father said.

Eli looked at his father. What well was he talking about? There was no well on their property. He looked at his grandfather. He seemed massive. He filled the porch. The glass in his hand was so tiny, the sun glinting on it, illuminating the liquid inside and melting the ice. Eli started to reach out to him, but the world spun around him. Trees and grass and leaves and branches. The sun cut through the canopy in splotches. Eli shook his head. And then his grandfather disappeared and his father was no longer working on the car. The porch and driveway were empty, and then gone altogether. Nothing but the forest remained.

Eli walked through the ferns and found Maggie lying on a fallen tree. "You okay?" he asked, touching her head.

"I feel terrible," Maggie said.

"Drink some water. Try to eat something."

Maggie wiped her face and sat up. "I can't hold anything down."

Eli nodded. "We can stop here for the night."

They set up only one tent and Eli started a fire. Maggie had some boxed rice and they cooked it, but neither of them ate much. Before sunset, they climbed into the tent. They wrapped their arms around each other and shivered with fever.

When Eli closed his eyes, he saw the trail and the trees and the leaves. Their image was burnt into his retinas from days of staring at them. He slipped into sleep still staring at the forest, his eyes fluttering under their lids.

Ben held the phone to his ear and played with the cord with his other hand. "Okay, well thank you," he said, hanging up.

He rubbed the back of his neck. He'd been calling ranger stations in Virginia, in the area where the boy had called from, all day, making sure they had the photo and were looking for Eli.

He spun in his chair. "Daryl," he called. He waited for a response. None came. "Daryl!" He heard some shuffling down the hall. A moment later, Daryl stuck his head through the door.

"What's up, boss?" he said.

Ben looked at him. His uniform was crumpled and hung off his body. "I'm going out to get some supper. I've got a list of ranger stations in Virginia I want you to call while I'm gone. Ask them if they have the flyer of the Sutton boy, and tell them he was spotted in their area not long ago."

Daryl nodded his head. "Sure thing." He started to leave.

"Oh, and Daryl?" Ben said.

Daryl turned back around.

"Get a uniform that fits. You look like a sack of crap."

Eli lay in the forest—paralyzed. Tree trunks like giants' legs grew from the earth, burst from the soil and shot toward the sky. Thousands of arms, covered in leafy fingers, opened and sucked up the air. Vines crawled across the forest floor and ferns lapped against the trees in waves.

A stone split the soil, rising out of it like a bubble through mud. It grew into the shape of a woman, of U`tlun'ta, her skin ashen and cracked, a gray splotch among the green. She reached out to Eli, reached for him with her pointed forefinger. Her other fingers were curled into a bony fist and held something, something that pulsed and squished black liquid between her fingers. A chickadee flew from the brush and landed on her hand. She swatted at the bird, but it flew away unharmed. Her mouth gaped, dripping mud. Her tiny dark eyes, set in stone sockets, were hypnotic.

A raven shrieked. U`tlun'ta glanced behind her and vanished as the sky above the canopy turned red. The bird continued to shriek and shriek. It grew closer, louder. Eli saw it fly overhead, a trail of flames and sparks burned behind it.

The forest shook. White light traced the trees and leaves and flowed through the bark. The leaves crumbled to dust and burned the ground where they fell. The limbs melted and the trunks blackened. The bird disappeared as the forest brightened. Eli could see nothing but a wall of blinding light. He began to gasp for breath, realizing that something pressed down on him, something sat on his chest. He tried to move, tried to push himself up, but he couldn't. Then two red slits opened, gleaming like tiny red suns. The Raven Mocker was on him, staring at him. He was there because Eli would be dead soon. He was there to eat his heart and steal his life.

Eli screamed.

Eli's eyes popped open and he gasped. The inside of the tent was dim with morning light. He heard Maggie vomiting outside.

They packed the tent. Eli ate the opened granola bar from the previous day, but nothing else. "Did you sleep?" he asked Maggie.

"A little. I had odd dreams," she said.

Eli only nodded.

The day started slow and didn't pick up pace. The forest was hot. It seemed to buzz with the heat. The birds were silent.

By early afternoon, they were beat again. Eli's legs felt weak, his back and neck stiff.

He heard water running in the distance and was thankful. They needed to refill their canteens. They hiked toward the sound, eventually coming to a sloping hill. They slipped down it like a slide. At the bottom, they stood on the bank of a river.

"What now?" Maggie asked.

Eli looked downriver. "We cross." A tree lay over the water like a bridge, suspended several yards above the river. "Then we'll stop on the other side and boil some water."

The tree's jagged roots, ripped from the earth, soil clinging to them, stuck into the air. Eli pulled himself onto the trunk. Maggie grabbed a root and tried to pull herself up, but it broke and she fell onto her butt. The wood was brittle and sponge-like. It crumbled at her touch, leaving her fingers covered in dust.

Eli reached down, offering his hand. She took it and he pulled her onto the tree. Its surface was smoothed by age and tiny holes were drilled into it. Where the bark had fallen off, zigzagging, twisting trails marked the wood. Something, termites or beetles perhaps, had lived there.

"I'm not sure about this," Maggie said. "It doesn't look very stable."

Eli stomped a few times and then jumped on the trunk. The tree bounced, but didn't break. "It's fine," he said.

They walked onto the tree. The water rushed underneath them. Mist rose into the air. The trunk grew narrower and wetter. Eli used the branches to keep his balance and glanced behind him to make sure Maggie was all right.

Halfway across the river, a crack echoed in Eli's ears. He turned and looked at Maggie. Neither of them moved for a moment. Sweat dripped down Maggie's face. Her eyes and mouth were wide with worry. Eli slowly turned, swallowed dryly, and took a shaky step. The trunk creaked as he set his foot down, shifting his weight.

Maggie reached out and touched his shoulder. He turned back to her and smiled. "It's all right," he said, taking another step. The tree felt soft under his foot. He reached for a branch to steady himself with, and the tree moaned, a low strangled noise that vibrated underfoot.

Then the trunk snapped. Eli felt the space under him open as the tree fell.

Maggie screamed as the wood slammed into the river.

The branch Eli was holding broke and he fell onto the trunk, gripping the soft wood. The tree turned as the water tried to drag it from the bank. Eli felt himself rolling with it. His weight shifted. He started to slip off the trunk, but his pack caught on a branch. It tore down the side, spilling the last of his food in the water, but stopping his fall.

He looked at Maggie. She gripped a large limb, panic plastered on her face.

Then the tree lodged against a rock and stopped moving. It was half in the water and half on the bank. Eli breathed for a second. His feet dangled just inches from the river.

"Hold on," Maggie said, still clinging to the branch. She reached for him, but the tree started to slip from the rock.

"Stay there," Eli yelled. Sweat and mist mixed on his skin. He tried to pull himself up, but his arms were weak and his pack was still caught. He twisted, trying to get it loose without moving the tree.

His grandfather's journal slipped through the tear in the side of his pack. He tried to catch it but it happened too quickly. He watched it splash into the river. He watched it float away. He felt like smashing something.

He jerked his pack loose and scrambled back onto the trunk of the tree. He looked downriver. The journal was out of sight. His body deflated. He couldn't believe it. He wanted to jump in the river and find the journal or drown trying.

Maggie grabbed his hand. "It's gone," she said. She pulled him up. They climbed the tree like a ladder and dropped onto the bank.

Eli fell on his back. How could this have happened, he thought.

Maggie dropped her pack and sat next to him. "I'm sorry," she said.

It wasn't her fault. It was his fault, everything was. Eli said nothing, though. He watched dragonflies and flowers blow in the wind. Other insects also drifted, floating on unseen waves. A hummingbird hovered above pink honeysuckle near the water. The sound of a jet echoed through the ravine. Dulled by distance, the white noise filled Eli's head, filled the forest.

Eli stared at a tree next to him. In the grain and the knots, in the swirls and the bark, he saw the Raven Mocker. He smiled at Eli, ready to burst from the bark any moment, and there was nothing Eli could do to stop him.

"Are you okay?" Maggie asked.

Eli turned to her.

"Your grandfather's journal ..."

"I—" Eli said. His words were gone, his mouth empty. He looked back at the tree. The Raven Mocker's face was no longer in it, but the forest seemed strange. It flowed. Light trickled through the leaves and bark. Everything seemed skewed. Disproportioned. Beneath the tree, a burrow was dug in the dirt. Something had lived there. Eli imagined the Yunwi Tsunsdi crawling into it at night. He wanted to climb inside, to burrow out of that world and into another one, a safer one. "I can't believe I lost it." He laid his head on Maggie's leg.

Maggie stroked his hair, touched his cheek, kissed his forehead. Then she started a fire on the rocks. They still needed water.

Ben came in from his afternoon patrol. As he entered the station, Daryl pulled up his email, hiding the game he'd been playing.

Ben said nothing. He just hung his hat.

Daryl flipped open a notepad. "I think I got some bad news, sir." Daryl bit his lip.

Ben rolled his eyes. "Well, let's have it."

"I got a call not long ago. A couple rangers south of Roanoke found some boxed food floating in a river."

Ben sighed. "Littering is quite a crime. What's it got to do with us, Daryl?"

"They also found a journal. It was in a plastic bag with a red handkerchief around it. The name on the inside cover is Jack Sutton."

Ben's shoulders sank. "It's got to be the boy's." He looked at the carpet. "Are they looking for a body?"

"They're scouting the river around where they found the journal."

"I guess I better drive out to the Sutton place," Ben said. He put his hat back on. What was he going to tell Dee? He struggled over it as he drove to her home. When he arrived, he got out of his car and looked up at the trees for a moment, collecting his thoughts. He walked up the porch steps and knocked on the door.

Dee opened it. Her eyes were red. She looked like she hadn't slept in a week.

"Afternoon, Dee," Ben said.

"Did they find him?" Dee asked.

Ben took a deep breath. "Dee, did Eli have a journal on him?" he asked.

Dee nodded. "He took Jack's, his grandfather's journal with him."

"Jack Sutton." Ben took a deep breath. "Some rangers found it near Roanoke."

"What does that mean?" Dee asked.

"Nothing yet. I just thought you should know. They're searching the area."

The water finally boiled. Eli watched the cleansing bubbles rumble in the pot. After a few minutes, Maggie removed the water from the flame and set it aside to cool. She opened Eli's pack. "Don't you have some duct tape in here?" she asked.

"Unless it fell in the water as well, yes. Why?" Eli watched her dig through his things.

She smiled thinly and removed the tape. "To fix your pack with." She pulled long strips of it off the roll, tearing it with her teeth. "You're not quitting now, are you?" She used the tape to cover the tear, stitch it closed.

Eli watched her work. She was right. He'd lost the journal, but he still had a goal. He picked up the roll of tape and tore a piece off. He handed it to Maggie.

"Thank you," she said, holding his gaze.

Eli leaned forward and kissed her. Then he turned to the pot of water.

As he topped off his second canteen, voices yelled to them over the noise of the river. Both Eli and Maggie turned. Two forest rangers stood a few dozen yards downriver, on the opposite bank.

"Stay there," one of the rangers yelled.

Maggie stood up and put on her pack. Eli looked up at her.

"Come on," she said. "We're not stopping. You lost the journal, but you still have your knife. We're going to make it to Mount Katahdin. You're going to carve your name in that tree."

Eli looked at the forest rangers. He felt tired and feverish.

"We're coming over to you," one of them said. They walked back into the woods.

Low limbs and brush shook as they passed. Between the leaves, Eli could see the rangers. Mist rose off the river and glimmered in the air. In a flash, Eli saw U`tlun'ta's stone-like skin moving through the trees. He wiped his face in disbelief. When he opened his eyes, the Raven Mocker was looking through the leaves at him. Eli blinked and the face was gone.

He looked at Maggie. "All right. Let's go."

They hiked up the ravine as fast as they could. The forest rangers yelled across the river at them. Eli and Maggie picked up their pace until they were out of sight.

As the sun set, they pressed on, afraid that if they stopped the rangers would catch up with them. The forest grew dimmer and dimmer until the darkness swept across them and the forest cooled. Eli pulled on his fleece and headlamp, and Maggie put on her jacket.

Eli walked through the darkness. His headlamp shot beams of light into the trees. Their limbs twisted toward the sky. A few stars shined through the canopy. Eli smiled.

Then something cooed in the distance. His smile dripped from his face. He looked behind him.

Maggie was gone.

Relief swept over Dee as Ben spoke to her through the phone.

"The rangers that found him had to backtrack to a footbridge and by the time they crossed the river he'd run off again," Ben said. "The other boy, the one who called you, his sister is with Eli. Anyhow, the rangers are sweeping the forest in the area, and ..."

The details all blurred together in Dee's mind. All that mattered was that her baby wasn't floating face down in the river somewhere.

Eli froze. "Maggie?" he called. No reply. A figure drifted through the trees. He swallowed. "Maggie?" he said, barely managing a whisper.

No response came. He set down his pack and pulled on his wrist rocket. He felt the stones in his pocket.

He saw a shape in the dark. "Who's there?" Eli asked. He aimed the sling into the black, pulling back the pocket that held the rock. "Maggie?" he called.

The figure moved across the beam of light. It was a woman, skin like stone, hair long and stringy, arms thin and wired with muscle. Eli blinked, but the woman remained. He pinched his eyes closed. When he opened them, she was gone. He lowered the wrist rocket. His fear was getting the better of him again.

Then he felt something touch his shoulder. He turned around and was face to face with U`tlun'ta's mouth. Her gums dripped mud; her teeth were yellow. Eli screamed and fell back, the rock tumbled from his sling. He closed his eyes, knowing that when he opened them she would be gone. But then he felt her hand grip his ankle and pull him through the grass.

She sang as she walked, as she pulled him. It was a language Eli didn't know, but he understood the song's meaning. "Liver, I eat it," she sang.

Eli opened his eyes and screamed. She turned and smiled at him. She pointed at him with her long finger, her other fingers curled into a fist, black muck dripping between them.

Eli kicked free and scrambled away. He ran into the darkness, leaving his pack on the forest floor. U`tlun'ta laughed behind him and then sang again, "Liver, I eat it." Eli's light shined through the trees as he sprinted, casting bobbing shadows into the forest. He waited for her to tackle him, but she didn't. Her voice grew farther away until only silence remained.

Eli stopped running. Sweat poured from his face. His eyes searched the forest. "Maggie!" he screamed, over and over.

Then he saw something move through the trees. He pulled another rock from his pocket and slipped it into his sling. "Maggie?" he called.

U`tlun'ta rushed out at him. Eli sucked in his breath, pulled the sling back, and let it go. The rock struck her chest and bounced off. She grabbed his arm and threw him into the dirt. The sling shot slid off his wrist. He scrambled for it as she pounced at him, her finger heading straight for his chest. Eli rolled out of the way and was up like lightning, sprinting, clutching the wrist rocket.

He slipped down a hill and rolled to a stop. He looked behind him, focusing his light where he had been. U`tlun'ta smiled at him and sang her song.

Eli screamed at her, a scream of fear and anger, an animal's scream. She faded into the darkness, but her singing remained. He turned and ran. His light flickered in all directions. He could still hear her singing and laughing behind him. It didn't grow any farther away, but it also didn't get any closer. The sound just hung somewhere behind him, like he was dragging her along with a rope.

Then his light shined on a shack, what probably used to be a farmhouse. He sprinted toward it, sucking in air. Suddenly, he realized it was his home. It was his home, but it was crumbling with age. He ran up the steps, up the porch where his grandfather used to sit, sipping iced tea. He looked through a window, shining his light inside. There was no one in it. Only dust and cobwebs filled the space.

U`tlun'ta sang in the distance. Eli couldn't run anymore. His lungs were bursting. He was out of energy. He tried the door. It wouldn't open. U`tlun'ta's singing grew closer. He kicked the door. It was as solid as the trunk of a tree. Then he remembered what his father had said. He'd told him not to play near the well. Off the porch, he shined his light on the ground. To his right, the earth disappeared, sank into a deep hole—an old well.

Eli rushed over to it. The pit was about eight feet wide and perhaps fifteen deep. U`tlun'ta sang. She was close. Eli positioned himself so the well was between him and her voice. He loaded a stone in his sling and turned off his light. Darkness covered him like a blanket. "Come and get me!" he yelled into the black. "Come and eat my liver!"

U`tlun'ta's singing stopped. Silence filled Eli's mind. It was worse than the singing. He wanted to turn on his headlamp. He wanted to shine it into the forest. But if he did that, he would give away the pit. "Come on!" he yelled.

He heard the crunch of leaves about a dozen yards away. He stepped a couple of feet back and to his left, trying to line himself up with the noise. "I'm right here, U`tlun'ta. I give up. You can have me." The crunching stopped. Eli swallowed.

In the darkness, U`tlun'ta screamed. It filled the forest with a cold sound, and caused Eli's spine to quiver. But he held his ground. Even as he heard her filthy feet sprinting toward him, he didn't move.

Then he heard a crash and nothing more. His heart pounded. He turned on his light and looked into the woods—nothing. He leaned toward the edge of the pit. U`tlun'ta lay at the bottom. Her chest rose and fell. Eli wiped the sweat from his brow. Her eyes opened. She smiled up at him and sang again.

Eli drew back the sling and fired the stone. It bounced off her chest. She laughed and pulled herself up. She pointed her long finger at him and sang her song. Black liquid squished between her fingers. There was something in her fist, something small and dark. Eli remembered the dream he had the previous night. The chickadee had landed on her closed hand. Perhaps it had been signaling him.

Eli took aim at her fist. He fired his stone. It whizzed into the well, missing her hand by inches.

U`tlun'ta screamed and clawed at the sides of the well with her open hand. Dirt rained down on her. She jumped up and tried to grab the top of the pit.

Eli loaded another stone. He held his breath. He aimed, following U`tlun'ta's movement. He thought of his father and grandfather. He let go of the sling and the rock flew. It hit her closed hand, right at the wrist, and shattered her grip. A tiny black heart, pumping mud, dropped to the ground. U`tlun'ta's eyes rolled up, and she fell over, dead.

Eli breathed and closed his eyes. He knew what was next. He had dreamt it. The Raven Mocker would swoop down on him from the sky in white fire. He looked up, but no bird called and no lightning struck.

"Eli?" Maggie's voice came from the woods.

He screamed back and ran toward her voice. His headlamp bounced yellow beams into the forest. Then he saw her, her hand shielding her face from the light. He rushed to her and hugged her.

"Where did you go?" she asked. "It's scary out here. You left me alone."

"What?" Eli said. "You disappeared."

"I told you I was going to be sick. I was puking in the woods," Maggie said.

Eli didn't remember that.

"When I came back, your pack was lying on the ground and you were gone."

"U`tlun'ta attacked me. Look at this," he said, pulling Maggie's hand. They walked back to where Eli had been. The ground was solid. There was no pit. His crumbling home was also gone. He shook his head at the trees.

"What are you looking for?" Maggie asked.

Eli stared into the forest. "Nothing ... I ... nothing."

"We need to stop," Maggie said. "Let's sleep a few hours and then we'll go."

They didn't set up a tent. They just unrolled their sleeping bags on the ground and crawled in them. Maggie fell asleep instantly. Eli lay awake, staring at the stars between the leaves. He couldn't understand. He remembered seeing U`tlun'ta so clearly. He shook his head. Nothing made sense. He drifted in and out of sleep until twilight gleamed in the distance.

The sun stretched just below the horizon. Eli imagined it waking, shaking the sleep from its eyes, and pulling itself into place. Through the trees he could see a violet glow that slowly grew to rose, to pink, to orange, to gold. The sky above him turned from black to blue. The stars faded away as the twilight turned to day.

The forest turned golden. Eli felt the light on his eyes, felt it warm his face. It seemed impossibly bright compared to the darkness of the night. He almost could feel the earth turn beneath him, carrying him into the morning.

As the light turned from gold to yellow and the moist night air began to warm, Eli heard the rumble of an engine. He sat up and looked into the trees. Not far away, he could see a dirt road. He shook Maggie awake and pointed toward it.

She rubbed her eyes. "What is it?"

Eli put his finger to his lips: quiet. The sound of rubber on gravel drifted through the trees. He slipped out of his sleeping bag and started rolling it up. Maggie did the same. As they stuffed their bags away, a pickup drove up the road. It read "State Forest Ranger" on the side.

Eli ducked down but the pickup stopped abruptly. He pulled on his pack, grabbed Maggie's hand. They ran through the brush and up a steep hill.

"Hey, boss," Daryl said. "Just got a call from a ranger near Roanoke, said they spotted Eli and the girl."

Ben sucked his teeth. "Why didn't they stop them?" he asked.

"They ran. Took off into the woods and up," Daryl read his notepad, "McAfee Knob. The rangers are heading for the top now. Said they'll call when they have more information."

Up and up, it seemed to never end. Eli felt weak, distant, confused. He glanced behind him. Maggie plodded along, but he didn't see or hear the rangers pursuing. He couldn't think. He wiped his face. All he knew to do was keep going, keep walking.

Eli and Maggie both breathed heavily as they crested the hill. The trees cleared and the world opened before them. Eli walked out onto a large stone ledge and surveyed the landscape. He stood, wavering a bit, staring at the scenery. He couldn't believe it. He pulled his compass out.

To the west, a large valley and mountain. To the north, cliffs. To the east, rolling blue ridges. It was just as his grandfather described. Eli walked to the edge of the ledge. Could this be where his grandfather sat and wrote his last journal entry? It wasn't Mount Katahdin, but it had to be the place. Everything was just as he described. If that was the case, then the tree would be directly behind him. Eli dropped his pack and ran into the trees.

"Where are you going?" Maggie said. She was swaying, her hair glued to her forehead with sweat.

Eli didn't answer. He scanned the trees. Then he saw it. A thick trunk with old scars on it. One scar was his father's name, the other his grandfather's. Eli put his hand on the tree, on the rough bark. He traced the names. He shook his head. The whole time—the whole time he thought his grandfather had hiked all the way to Maine.

Eli pulled out the pocketknife. He felt its blade. He pressed it into the tree. Digging the knife into the bark, he cut his name deep into the tree to make sure it would stay, make sure it would last as long as his father's and grandfather's.

When he finished, he looked behind him. Maggie was sprawled in the leaves and the grass. Eli's eyes drifted to the sky. The morning sun shined down on his face. He could feel each individual ray. He felt a breeze push him over. The soil was soft, sponge-like. He felt water bubble out of the earth and surround him, carry him away. Then he heard laughter, the laughter of the Yunwi Tsunsdi. It filled the space between, the space where matter became nothing, filled his mind with smiles and life. Behind the laughter, he was vaguely aware of a man approaching him. He looked up and saw the face of his father staring back.

This was it, he thought. He was dead. Whatever sickness he'd contracted from the water had run its course and killed him. He was moving into the afterlife, the world of spirits. He waited for the Raven Mocker to come.

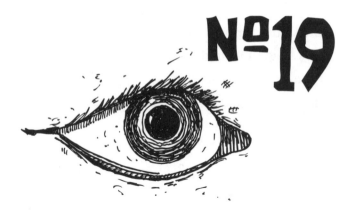

Eli woke up in the hospital. The room slowly came into focus, and then he felt his mom's arms around him, smelled her familiar smell, and heard her voice. His eyes watered as she hugged him.

"I'm sorry," he said.

Tears burst from his mom's eyes and she laughed. "You better be."

They held each other for what felt like an eternity, and Eli was okay with it.

His mom was the one to break the embrace. She pushed him back and touched his face. "The nurses said you were a mess when they brought you in: dehydrated, delirious, covered in mud." She smiled at him and wiped her eyes. "You were with some girl, too?"

Eli's eyes opened wide. "Is she okay?"

His mom nodded. "Outside of a little Giardia, she's fine. She's just down the hall. You're both on antibiotics." His mom smiled at him. "What were you doing out there?"

Light poured through the window and into the room. Eli shook his head. The night had passed, but he didn't know what to say.

His mom sighed but smiled. She reached into her purse and took out the journal, still wrapped in the silk handkerchief. She set it on the bed.

Eli touched the silk, pushed it aside, and looked at the journal. It was intact. "Mom?" he asked.

"What is it?" she squeezed his arm.

"Was there a well on our property when I was young?"

"That's an odd question, but yes. There was. Your father had it filled in. He was always so afraid you'd fall in there. Why do you ask?"

Eli shook his head and touched the journal, the handkerchief covering the back of his fingers. He felt the combination of silk and old leather. It felt like nothing he'd ever felt before. His blindfold was off, and he could see. There was nothing to fear. The only ghosts on the Appalachian Trail belonged to his father and grandfather.

Before Eli was released from the hospital, he walked down the hall and found Maggie's room. A smile spread across her face as he entered. "Eli!"

Her mom, a woman like a wall, sat on the other side of Maggie's bed. "This is the fool boy you run off with? I ought to slap you right here, young man. Filling my daughter's head with nonsense, running off—"

"Stop it," Maggie said to her mom. "It wasn't his fault."

Her mom put a hand up, shook her head, and sucked what seemed to be all the air in the room up into her nostrils and then blew it out her mouth.

Maggie rolled her eyes. "Are you leaving soon? How much longer are they keeping you? They said I should stay another night."

"They're releasing me," Eli said. "My mom and I are leaving." Eli glanced at Maggie's mom. Then he pulled out the red silk handkerchief.

"How did you—"

"The rangers. They found it," Eli said.

Maggie rubbed the silk between her fingers and Eli did the same. Eli set it on her bed. "I want you to have it."

Maggie reached out and took his hand. She squeezed his fingers and smiled.

When Eli got home, he stood in his room. He felt foreign among the bed and the blankets, the desk and the drawers, the television and the books. He no longer felt confined, though. He set his grandfather's journal on the desk and reached into his pocket. He pulled the scrap of paper out that Maggie had written her phone number and email address on. He set it on the desk as well.

He lay on the bed. He looked at the ceiling for a moment and then closed his eyes. He saw the trail and the trees, smelled the leaves, felt the soil underfoot and the sweat on his palms. But he no longer had a destination. He no longer had a goal, a purpose on that path.

He opened his eyes and looked at his grandfather's journal. He could create another purpose. He could give his experience to his children and grandchildren, just like his grandfather had done.

He sat down at the desk and dug through a drawer. He pulled out a notebook, found a pen, and started writing.